DOORWAY TO FREEDOM

21 Lessons that will change your reality

Barry Elwin-Jones

tara press

Doorway to Freedom
Barry Elwin-Jones

Tara Press
(Trade division of India Research Press)
Flat No.6, Khan Market, New Delhi - 110 003
Ph.: 24694610; Fax : 24618637
www.indiaresearchpress.com
contact@indiaresearchpress.com; bahrisons@vsnl.com

2010

ISBN 13 : 978-81-8386-028-4

Printed for *India Research Press* at Focus Impressions, New Delhi-110003

I asked for clarity of vision and hearing so that I may Serve better.

And four angels appeared.

The first angel said: "I give you Wisdom by opening your third eye so that you may see the suffering of others and have the insight to help them in their best interest."

The second angel said : "I give you Light so that you may see your way and draw to you those who cannot see in the darkness."

The third angel said: "I give you Heart so that you will experience love and peace and spread it amongst others."

The fourth angel said: "I give you a Golden Sword to defeat the enemies of Truth and protect those who are weak and confused. Carry these blessings with you always."

CONTENTS

Lesson [illegible] [illegible]

The Mind [illegible]

[illegible] I allow the power of Love [illegible] [illegible] [illegible] [illegible] [illegible] [illegible] [illegible]

Lesson [illegible] [illegible]

[illegible] [illegible]

Your [illegible] the [illegible] [illegible] [illegible] What [illegible] [illegible] [illegible]

Lesson [illegible] [illegible]

[illegible] [illegible]

[illegible] [illegible]

[illegible] 119

[illegible]

INTRODUCTION

The structure of the book is designed to take you progressively through lessons incorporating affirmations and meditations that all link together to assist you to a higher understanding or change of mind. Do not rush the lessons, take your time to assimilate and understand them as best you can. Rushing through lessons will give you mental dyspepsia, hardly a dangerous situation, but avoidable. Take the attitude that you have had thousands of lifetimes to reach this point, so why rush? Honour yourself with careful preparation. Each lesson is a lifetime of work. You will revisit different lessons many times as you grow. Once you have been through them, you may decide to move through each individual lesson in an order to suit you at this time. The lessons could take you months if done carefully on the first run through. In my classes with students these lessons sometimes take five to six months to begin a comprehensive change in their life. In just one day, all the lessons can present themselves in your life.

I have attempted to impart some of the major lessons we all need to understand at the deepest level. They are not mind fodder, but spiritual lessons that take us to the very essence of learning, which is experience beyond words. In other words to have insights and find the truth within us. Stripped of unnecessary words they are designed to provide direct experience to the reader, devoid of flowery language that stimulates the intellect but does little for the heart.

I know that if you apply what is written in this book, you will change and grow. This I can promise you. And you can return over and over to the lessons and continue to learn and grow. It is as if the book keeps changing with your growth. It is, in fact, your understanding that grows and continues to perceive new realities that were unavailable to you in the past.

ALLOWING TIME

It is not only your consciousness that changes, your body assimilates mental changes as well. So be kind to yourself and set a flexible programme for self-healing. Don't beat up on yourself if you take time out. Time for assimilation and rest from personal growth is as important as the actual work time. This will enable you to return to your work refreshed and enthusiastic, to learn more about yourself.

Please do not make your quest for spiritual enlightenment hard work to the point of becoming sick of it. Be as light as you can with it. Know that you have had thousands of lifetimes and there are countless more. You are eternal. That should be enough time! Relax and enjoy the road, create happiness and joy wherever you go; that in itself spreads light on the planet.

Be assured that all sincere seekers of truth draw to themselves people and events that are needed for growth. Do not struggle, it's as easy as having the desire in your heart, the divine plan will organise the rest. When you feel tired and ready to give up, look to the spiritual teachers who came to show us the way for inspiration; The Dalai Lama, Sathya Sai Baba, Nelson Mandela, the Pope, Rev. Billy Graham, Mother Teresa, Jesus, Buddha. There are people all over the planet doing the work of Truth in their own special way. Do not exclude yourself, you are a carrier of the Light, too.

Some Light workers are not well-known, others are high profile. Your destiny is to enlighten yourself through your own efforts. You are well- equipped to do it and you will succeed.

NATURE OF THE HUMAN SPIRIT

During our journeys together, we have waged war on each other, stolen from each other and perpetrated all manner of horrendous acts upon each other. Sometime, we must say stop! The brave will stop first and endure the fear of others knowing that they are showing their Light to the world. This path is not for the faint-hearted ; it takes great courage to show who you really are.

When my heart hurts, yours will too. That is the very nature of our connectedness. You and I have been around for millions of years and we will be together forever. When will we begin to see the Truth in each other and let go of our egos so we may live the life that we both want so badly? Your needs are mine, this is a basis for spiritual growth without fear.

I ask you, my sisters and brothers, to join me on the inner journey to higher states of consciousness so that we may put aside our fears together. Many have shown the way and many more need to follow it. In our own small way, we help light up the world with our hearts and together we can overcome the fear entrenched on this planet.

Light and Truth will prevail because that is our true nature. No matter how well we hide our Divinity, we must eventually break through our delusions and free ourselves. This step takes courage because we fear to turn our backs on what appears real to us in exchange for Truth, which we have not experienced. Our fear urges us to fully experience the new before letting go of the old. In this instance we must trust, believing the divine plan is filled with love and cares for every soul.

Our world has been steeped in fear since we chose it to be so. By choosing the opposite as our reality, millenniums of darkness and ignorance will give way to the Light in our hearts. The work you do on enlightening yourself helps other souls by raising the planetary vibration, bringing about gentle opportunities for change in those around you.

We change our hairstyles, our jobs, our lovers, our husbands, our wives, our place of living, our country, our cars, even our eating habits. Where has that taken us? It really is time to address where the real change needs to happen. That is what this book is about, facilitating change.

Our nature is to give and receive love. No other activities are as important as the giving and receiving of love. In our life we experience different expressions of love ; from different teachers we are shown how to express love in wide and varied ways.

Love is taught to us as giving. Giving is believed to be the ultimate expression of love. And it is. However, when distortion has been learned, giving becomes a self-aggrandising act to feed our own ego. We sometimes demonstrate love to others only to meet the criteria learned through distorted thinking. Giving love is no longer a natural process without effort or self-judgement when the ego is employed, subtle as it may be.

Expressing love is the essential nature of a Soul. The absolute energy of a Soul is love. The human spirit made manifest on the earth plane reflects and directs this love. There is no need to consciously do anything with love, it just is. Just as light radiates for all to use and see, a Soul need only exist to illuminate the world. All other acts are unnecessary. You are, there is nothing to prove. The light of love radiates from the Soul effortlessly when unhindered.

Love can be expressed without words or actions. Love does not have to be wilfully or consciously demonstrated.

Love is a state of being, not an emotion. A beautiful bird does not have to express anything for us to fully appreciate its beauty. A beautiful being is just that, and it is known by all who come into its energy field. If we believe that we must consciously demonstrate love, then we stifle the natural flow that is already there. The fear of not being loving enough completely blocks the natural expression of who you are. When you know you are Love, you no longer need to think about who you are, or feel a need to demonstrate it.

The nature of the human spirit is Love, expressed through forgiveness, joy and happiness. Here we see the ultimate expression of the inner Truth. To lose contact with our true nature is to choose fearful thoughts and generate energy around us that blocks out our Light. The cause of all unhappiness is fear. Love is the doorway to complete fulfilment and expression of our true nature. Nothing can bring unhappiness to us except fear, a totally unnatural state of being. We fear everything that is perceived through the ego, especially our guilt. From our past, we judge others and ourselves in the present, perpetuating fear and guilt, surrounding ourselves in darkness, not allowing our Light or that of others to shine. This is opposed to our loving nature that has within it an unlimited supply of forgiveness. Only fear stops forgiveness.

Your true nature has no limits or boundaries in Spirit. The universe is you and you are the universe; you reflect all. Yet you fear loss of what you cannot lose. You cry out for a gift that you have already as your birthright. You believe what your own manufactured fear tells you, rather than accepting what an all powerful, loving Spirit has already presented you with from the beginning.

Our nature is to fully express our Inner Light. In this expression we will dissolve fear in others and ourselves. Where light shines darkness cannot exist. In expressing our true nature it is necessary to let go of fear. This first step seems huge. When a child first jumps off a springboard at the swimming pool and experiences the exhilaration of breaking through the fear, he wonders why it took so long to jump. Our own wall of fear prevents us from jumping into life. The exhilaration we experience when showing our loving and forgiving nature is an endless experience of the heart. A freedom that is magical, yet real and everlasting. Knowing that we are allowing our true Self to shine through.

The only constant state we can have is the experience of Self. Self requires endless growth through experience, constantly expanding our consciousness through realisations derived from learning. Our uniqueness is seen in the ability to be conscious of our thoughts. We can observe our internal reactions to external events.

The effect on us is brought about by our reactions to our thoughts. Every being reacts differently, thereby creating their own reality.

Searching for consistency, we find that the experience of our true nature is, and will always be, found on our inner journey. There is no end to the experiences and realities in our Universe as we are the centre of that Universe. The light of Love is the pathway down which we find consistency and transformation.

The inner experience of self brings peace. Our ever-changing experiences challenge us to remain in that peace, embracing love and not fear. This allows us to see the Truth in all situations. We are enlightened when we always see Truth in all things and events. Fear cannot exist as we approach the enlightened state. At this point effort disappears and our true nature takes over. The struggle has ceased. Fear must go so that Love can fully express itself.

Continued reaction to negative thoughts, from which we perceive terrible future events, is usually unfounded; we are listening to the controlling ego. A person who is victim to ego's fear suffers needlessly for far longer than necessary. The lead up to the dreaded event can be longer than the event itself, which is nearly always less traumatising than the expectation of it. We can reduce our suffering by living and enjoying life in the moment. We know that physical death is inevitable, but we do not know the hour it will come, and we do not spend our entire life stressing about it.

So as experiences of life approach us, judgement through the ego's fear needs to be abandoned. Being non-judgemental and letting events play out their energy without physical or psychic interference will allow the karma to present itself as it was meant to. Only then will the Truth be seen. The best result possible is brought about by love not fear. Fear and judgement will blind you to the truth – love will let you see clearly what you need to learn.

Our nature is to be loving and joyful, so why do we deviate from that path? As fear blinded us to our true nature, we became truly lost. Seeing ourselves as a separate entity from the One, we became fearful. Believing that we needed to grasp and profit to survive, we lost our true nature in fear. If we all took care of each other, want in the world would give way to love, and fear would become a bad dream.

Most of my life has been spent looking inwards, not for spiritual values, but for self-centred reasons. Fear of loss had me always grasping for personal gain. The habitual thinking of "what's in it for me" was my God and driving force. An unwillingness to share my innermost thoughts and feelings was a symptom of my darkest days. In this state of fear, lies roll off the tongue, not for the sake of it, but to cover up the insecurity hidden within. Then we add some more guilt for good measure. How wonderful it would be to turn back the clock to make amends for our sins. However, that is not the way of things. We must learn to forgive others and ourselves and move on.

The corrections we make in our behaviour is our turning back of the clock. Evolving into loving human beings that live in Light and Truth gives us the opportunity to erase past actions. All our actions, present and future , must be done willingly, with love and service to human kind, with devotion to the Divine. Only with a happy heart in service to our world can we cleanse our past.

By serving your chosen partner and fulfilling their needs, you will be supplied with all your spiritual lessons. By serving others with love, your opportunities for growth abound. The lessons may be hard, but your inner growth will be great. The love that your partner returns will fill your heart. But if the love you seek is from without, then you are looking in the wrong direction. Your reward for service comes from within.

TO UNDO THE PAST YOU MUST RELEARN IN THE PRESENT

Life is about interacting with others. The lessons are about interacting with yourself through thoughts, emotions, words and actions. With great effort and persistence, we can overcome what appears to be impossible; controlling our thoughts, words and actions. Our judgements colour our thoughts, which in turn gives rise to emotion which colours our words and influences our actions. All of this can be controlled by us, but rarely are we mindful enough to ensure we retain our peaceful state and not hurt other souls.

PATIENCE AND LOVE

You will return to these lessons many times. True forgiveness is not attained quickly, a huge letting go is required. In degrees, over time, as the love grows in your heart it brings you to the doorway of true forgiveness. The blossoming of love gradually overpowers the fear in us and, sure that we are completely loved, we will merge consciously with the beloved Divine as it is ordained to be.

The best way to obtain the most benefit from this lesson and the following ones is to find a quiet part of your home, put up the "do not disturb sign" and take the phone off the hook. This is your special healing time - do not permit interruptions. The minimum duration should be at least one hour, two is better. It is a small ask of yourself and of your partner or family. A true forgiveness session takes hours not minutes and you may need to repeat it a number of times before it is done.

APPLYING THE PRINCIPLES

Apply what you have learnt on a daily basis—this is where you find out how much courage you have. Putting the principles to work means facing people who know you well and changing yourself in their eyes. How we acted out our roles in the past is usually quite different from how, with hindsight, we would like to have done. Now is the opportunity for you to become who really you are. Change comes as we release fear. Over and over again, I witness those students in my classes who apply themselves making great progress and blossoming with joy and love. This enlightenment comes about through letting go of what you really are not and embracing who you really are. There is nothing we need to add to ourselves but an awful lot to let go of.

PREPARATION

DESIRE

With learning, the task at hand may, at first, seem impossible. Then, gradually, we have little realisations inside that result from our efforts. These realisations encourage us to press on. The human spirit is resilient and persistence is needed. Persistence with anything we need or want to achieve, is fuelled by a secret ingredient. That ingredient is called desire. Before you can attain anything in this life, whether physical or spiritual, desire must be there. If you did not have it you would not be reading this book. A student said to me in class one day: "I have no personal desires. I have surrendered myself to God." My answer was," If you had no desire, you could not have surrendered to God. Your continuing desire is to let God work through you. Desire will be with you always as you desire to become one with God in the ultimate union."

THE TESTS OF LIFE

While working through the lessons, you will become aware of "tests" that come your way. These tests have always been in your life, you have just not seen them before. View these tests as a wonderful opportunity to practise the skills that will take you to self-mastery. Knowledge alone will not take you there. Application of spiritual principles to your life will see you evolve, eventually to become a master of self, our very purpose in life.

I am not claiming this book will take you to complete self-mastery. My claim is that by diligently applying these principles in your life, you will become free of much that now binds you. No book or teacher can do anything for you that you do not earnestly desire for yourself. Like you, I am a student of self-mastery. I believe when we join with the Divine in the final act of union, in pure Consciousness, we have achieved. Until then, it's a case of student helping student.

THE INNER STRUGGLE

I tell every class of my students that as you apply the principles in your life, many issues from the past will re-surface to be dealt with. It is as if your new consciousness has given the Divine the go-ahead to start a clearing up. Any soldier who has experienced combat will tell you that the fighting becomes the fiercest just before the end of the battle. When you think things are getting too much for you, it is time to increase the effort, to "hang in there". Love will always win out ; Love may appear to lose the battle, but it will win the war.

This is not a battle to hang on but a battle to let go. We make it a battle but it does not have to be this way. The inner struggle is between the ego and us. Our ego will not go quietly, it has lived with us a long time. The tenant in our attic will fight the eviction notice to the bitter end.

RENOVATING THE ATTIC

The world is full of egotistical people who lack the fundamentals of self-mastery. These people, by choice, live in a spiritual vacuum. They remain in this existence where the ripples of life are not allowed to touch their reality, to disturb their intellectual calm. They appear in control, very "together people," hiding behind accumulated knowledge and a good intellect. I know, because I was one of them. When my world crashed around me, I was not a pretty sight. With hindsight, I thank the Divine every day for demolishing me so the rebuilding job could be undertaken. Reconstruction is an ongoing project.

WATCHING OURSELVES GROW

There is the story of the yogi who spent a lifetime meditating in a cave and appeared to have attained the ultimate peace. On his first venture into the busy market place, he was jostled and elbowed a few times. He lost 25 years of work as his anger rose and he could not control it.

You and I have the most wonderful opportunity, in relationships, families and workplaces, to grow. In other words, the market place of life is where self-mastery is to be won and held. We can test ourselves on our own progress by the minute and hour. There are no nasty surprises at the end; we know before we are tested how we are growing. You do not need to be a yogi or highly educated person to win the prize, we are all equally qualified and there is a first prize for every soul. Your guide for the journey is within your own heart. When listened to carefully, your life becomes more beautiful every day. Empower the Light within, let no one else have your power. Your channel is direct.

As you progress with these lessons, the contemplations take you to a new state of consciousness, or more correctly, you perceive things differently. This becomes part of your state of mind and goes beyond words. When this happens, a contemplation has taken up residence as an insight, and is part of you. A string of words has lead to an altered state of mind;you have become that which was once foreign to you. Each contemplation is written to be uplifting and spiritually enhancing.

FOLLOW THESE STEPS TO GET THE MOST FROM YOUR SESSIONS

- Use a comfortable chair or bed.
- Take time to prepare your space exactly the way that you like it. Burn oils and light candles for atmosphere and cleansing of the space.
- Prepare yourself by bathing immediately before beginning.
- Make sure you are comfortable and warm.
- Wear loose, comfortable clothing.
- Apply appropriate aromatherapy oils to your body if available.
- Follow whatever spiritual rituals you enjoy to bring in loving and supportive energy. Prayer and meditation create sacred space. Do whatever feels right for you.
- Dedicate this session to the inner Light and let go of all experiences that happen. Know that you are safe and protected.
- You may wish to ask Buddha, Jesus, or some other teacher to be with you. You do not have to ask the Divine to be with you, as you have never been apart and never will be.
- Sit and open your heart and feel the Love. Take a few minutes.
- Read the lesson slowly and carefully a number of times.

THE FOUNDATION

UNIVERSAL LAWS WORK FOR ALL

I have begun the lessons in this book with what some may feel is advanced learning. But I look at it this way; even though the laws for manifesting are potent in their simplicity, there is a need to be aware of them and study them in conjunction with the lessons. At first you may say, "I know this already." Well take it from me, I knew these laws for over forty years since about 18 years of age. However, I did not know them in the sense of seeing them work in front of my eyes. Because they are so powerful, sometimes I struggled to believe what I was manifesting. Do not let your ego deceive you into thinking that they do not work, because they do. There is no room for doubt.

A WARNING

The conscious or unconscious misuse of Universal Law brings its own karma. Highly successful people in all fields of endeavour use these laws. How you use them is your decision. To use them for the good of all and to apply these laws for your own spiritual growth with the intent to help others through the medium of your spiritual enlightenment is the highest use of the laws.

One-day seminars are built up around this single page, here you have the undiluted essence. Don't be fooled by their apparent simplicity. Use them with love and dedication to the inner Light always. Have absolute belief that they will work.

WHY THE FOUNDATION?

To achieve spiritual growth and ultimately your own self-mastery, it is absolutely necessary to understand what your mind is manifesting moment by moment. To blindly work hard on your self and at the same time to sabotage your own efforts, is a tragedy.

THE FIRST STEP

Become an observer of the workings of your mind and reject all thought processes that are in any way negative or destructive by using the universal laws for manifestation to negate and replace destructive thought patterns. There are many excellent publications available on this subject, add them to your self-help library. Meditation is important when wanting to observe how your mind works.

TEMPER ALL THOUGHTS, WORDS AND ACTIONS WITH LOVE

Within the principles of manifestation you will evolve your own techniques for holding positive energies around you and directing positive loving energy (thought patterns) outwards to others and situations. You need to know the laws of how things come into being and behold, you can then change things. Remember that unconditional love neutralises incoming energy forms that are not harmonious with love energy. All other rituals for protection are based on fear of being harmed in some way. It is time to take back your power and know that you are part of the Divine plan. There is no place for fear in your life.

LESSON 1

Laws Of Manifestation

CHANGING REALITIES

Much has been written about various magical processes that will take us somewhere where we will experience a different reality. This concept does not stand up to Universal Law. We are in charge of our own experience through our consciousness. We will experience other realities only after we change our mind. Only then is it possible to experience anything other than what we are now.

AN EXAMPLE

Go and sit in a public park near a beautiful bed of flowers, or choose some other magnificent location. Watch people passing by carefully. Some will stop at the flowers and enjoy them, taking time to smell and touch, soaking in all the wonder and beauty. Some walk by with no more than a casual glance. Others will not see them at all, and if questioned later will say, "what flowers?"

A person's state of mind determines their experience. Unless you and I have done the work, cleaned up our thoughts, words and actions we cannot experience other than where we are now.

KNOW WHAT YOU WANT FIRST

Be very clear about what it is you feel you need, before manifesting it. Once a third dimensional situation is happening it requires a lot of undoing if you decide you no longer want it around. I manifested a series of events consciously and deliberately in my life and paid a heavy price for my efforts, so be careful. Consider your actions carefully. Ensure that what you manifest is good for everyone. If it is a selfish manifestation, you will soon want to be rid of it but it will stay longer than you would like.

THE GREATEST GOOD COMES FROM SELFLESS ACTIONS

This transient world can supply to us, through our current consciousness any experience that we wish to have. After many lifetimes we find we still do the same things, make the same mistakes, suffer the same emotional pain. All these experiences have come to us by our conscious or unconscious use of the universal laws of manifestation. They cannot come any other way. This universe is not run by accident. By knowingly using the laws for the good of everyone, you can change your experience. When you care for your sisters and brothers, your needs will be looked after in ways you never thought possible

THREE LITTLE WORDS

Honesty. The honest person radiates a strength that has clarity like the freshness in the air on a clear frosty morning. Their energy field is clear and open, non-threatening, giving a feeling of trust and dependability.

Purity. The person who displays purity in thought, word and action summons respect from all that come near. The holy energy that manifests around this person is angelic in nature, strong but soft and filled with love.

SELFLESSNESS. The person who displays selflessness generates in their energy field devotion to the inner Light and Universal Law. The ego is transcended through service to the universe and its children.

Before manifesting anything in your life read the three little words first and take them into your consciousness so that they become you.

BENEFITS OF LIVING SPIRITUALLY

The body/mind experience is a direct reflection of our chosen state of consciousness. As we absorb the *three little words* into our beliefs, our body/mind relationship begins to change. Changing our way of thinking brings change to every cell in our body. Negative or fearful thinking cannot exist in the same consciousness as these Love-based principles of living. Bring these words into your everyday life and begin to live them as best you can. Be ready for the ego's reaction, it will not give in easily. Be gently persistent with yourself. With everything you do honour who you are. These words to live by were given to me by a teacher we all love on the other side of the veil. One day you and I will master all three.

Another benefit of living spiritually is a strength that develops within and around us. There is a purpose about people who live spiritually. They seem to stand still yet accomplish everything they need to. Amid the calmness they radiate is a controlled urgency to get things done. When things do not go the way they planned they suffer no stress, but accept that all is as it should be, and that energy expended has its purpose. They do not hold onto their actions or to people they have helped. When they feel anger, they control it and experience it; it is soon gone, and there is no guilt afterwards. By honouring themselves they do not allow anyone to abuse them on any level. By honouring themselves they see themselves in every other soul and extend to others every consideration.

A great inner strength comes from accepting spiritual values which change your consciousness. As the transient world lessens its hold over you a new, more powerful energy releases within you. Many call it the Holy Spirit. Divine consciousness, Clear Light, Universal Oneness. It does not matter what you call it, you will still feel it. A primal connectedness that we have buried is again revealed. By letting go of the old, we make room for the new. Or, by letting go of the new, the old and truthful ways can re-emerge.

PRINCIPLES OF MANIFESTATION

1. Energy Follows Mind. Therefore to concentrate energy into any given area is to "think' about this already being done. There is no room for doubt. Doubt instantly weakens the result or nullifies it completely. When we love someone there is no doubt in our mind and love is experienced instantly.

   The key is in the knowing that it is already done. In spirit, the result is already there before you have completed the thought.

   Because we have not learned to manifest our desires into third dimensional reality does not mean that they have not already manifested in spirit. They have. If we do not believe this then we cannot believe that healing energies manifest into the third dimension. Yet, we know they do. *So, energy follows thought.*

2. Thought. By focusing our thoughts on any place or *person, energy related to that thought (corresponding vibrations) will manifest at that point.* The result depends entirely on the type and quality of thought. As this becomes clear to us, paying attention to our thoughts takes on a new meaning and significance. Control of what we think about becomes very important, not only for ourselves

but for the whole of humanity. Our mind controls us. On our path to self-mastery, controlling thought is the first and most important victory over the mind. To ensure success, release the thought completely. To continue to labour over it will hold back energy and weaken the effect. A clear powerful thought with all the elements within it needs a split second only, then release it. The next time you think about your desired manifestation see it, hold the thought, it is done! Do not get involved in the details; it is done, completed, finished. Hold that thought and know it to be true. Expect it to come into being. *Have no doubt.*

3. Desire. is the fuel that determines the power or energy intensity of the thought you are projecting. If desire is missing there is no fire or core energy. The will power cannot switch into action when desire is missing. Having no desire stops us from being successful in any part of our lives. This ingredient is often overlooked; it is most important that desire is stimulated. If you do not want to manifest anything at all in your life, then you have no need for desire.

4. Will Power. is the conduit down which we channel the thought, coupled with the desire which is the fuel that makes the will strong and single pointed. You can liken the will to a pipe, the thought is the water and the desire is the pump that pushes the water to its destination.

5. Balance and Dedication. The final ingredient is balance. A harmonious balance of the three (Thought, Desire, Will) with unshakeable faith that it is already in Spirit, will manifest the desired result. Bring it into being. *Temper each thought with love and dedicate the activity to the Divine Consciousness.*

In this lesson are the keys to unlimited power, use it with love always. These laws apply to healing, telepathy, or anything else you may want to apply them to.

Healing can happen instantly, there is no need for protracted rituals when you have mastered the laws. You now have the knowledge. Simple yes, easy no. Doubt is the destroyer; it comes from the fearful ego.

LESSON 2

Forgiveness
The Doorway To Freedom

ENLIGHTENMENT CANNOT ENTER THROUGH A CLOSED DOOR

Forgiveness is the doorway to enlightenment or love consciousness, because without mastering forgiveness you cannot move on. It will always be the anchor that holds you back. Sooner or later you must forgive, for your own sake. Lack of forgiveness is a poison in your system that will rob you of your spiritual life. If you hate one soul you will never be able to love another completely. The poison will pollute your experience of love with everyone and everything in life. Lack of forgiveness spills over into other aspects of your life and stains your experiences.

When the time comes for true forgiveness, open yourself to your Light and invite the Universal Spirit to enter, to cleanse the cellular memory of all the negative energy stored in there. Dissolve with love the patterns you hold about others that you have not forgiven. The strength of the vibrations at this time can make your ego or logical mind have fearful thoughts.

Remember, we were created to experience perfection and beauty. When the Spirit meets our darkness, things happen in our best interest. Do not judge the situation, let it be.

WE CANNOT HATE ONE SOUL AND LOVE ANOTHER

For our own sakes we need to forgive one another; to be kind and considerate to each other and show tolerance. When we do not forgive, we poison our being with dark energies that foster anger that we then suppress and deny. This dishonouring of ourselves brings emotional pain that destroys our quality of life. Every experience that comes to us is filtered through this unforgiving attitude, thereby diluting our experience of the joy of being alive.

My dear friends, with our tongues we speak both praises and curses. We praise the Lord and Father, and we curse people who were created to be like God, and this isn't right.James 3:9-.0

THE LOSS OF SPIRITUAL LIFE

Vague shadows lurk in consciousness and drain our energy. The dullness of our experience robs us of our spirituality. We know there must be more, but we can never fully experience what we feel we should. The shadows from our lack of forgiveness keep our spiritual light from shining, preventing us from fully experienceing who we are.

HONOURING THE LESSONS

The longer we hold hard, unforgiving thoughts, the weaker our Light becomes, and consequently, the deeper the hurt from our own dishonouring of ourselves. Anger grows, no matter what the perceived sin is against us. Eventually forgiveness is the only doorway to freedom. All denial and suppression must be removed so that our Spirit is free and our heritage of a full and joyous spiritual life is realised while still on the earth plane. Unforgiveness is the state that divides and separates spiritual beings' experience of physical life. The damage is self-inflicted. The person who does not forgive is the victim of their own anger and does little or no damage to their perceived enemies. The people closest to them become secondary victims. As they weave their karmic web they draw others into their dance, intensifying and complicating a wonderful and simple experience. However, the dance, is one of learning and growth, so to judge it as wrong would be another misperception of the Truth. In all of life, options are open to us. The choice of how we learn is ours. And no matter how it appears to others, it is our choice. As we watch others learning, we must honour that person and the path of learning that they have chosen too. Judgement is not the way. Love and tolerance will open the door to Spiritual freedom.

FACING OUR GREATEST FEAR

Pain in the heart is the energy of love pushing against a blocked emotion contained there. Forgiveness shakes our very foundation and belief that we are the victim and that we are righteous in our anger. This belief pattern must go if we are to progress. Lack of forgiveness keeps us on the path of self-destruction. Justification of our behaviour is the indicator that we are out to convince others that we have a right to be angry, and hatred of another soul is completely justifiable because of what they did to us. Justification and self-elevation that puts us above others is the most divisive and destructive path that the ego takes us on.

By not forgiving, we are pushed further from our Light than at any other time. Because anger and hatred are the opposite of love, festering inner wounds will not heal and allow us to move forward until the door of forgiveness is reached. At this moment, depending on the intensity of the experience, the strongest person can cry and shiver like a frightened child deep in the experience of a nightmare. You see the wrongs you have done to yourself. Yet the gentle prompting from our own divinity never lets us forget who we are; it is the inner voice of sanity. This voice is our link to the Inner Light, our conscience, the whispering of our Soul. The comforting words of our True self, our True being, and the doorway through which enlightenment will come. The fear perpetuated by the ego needs to be faced and seen for the illusion that it is, which has robbed us of our spiritual life.

HONOURING OUR MAGNIFICENCE

When we stand before the Light of who we are, and prepare to allow this Light to enter our darkness, the fear of lifetimes accumulated in our cellular memory trembles in a way that defies description. The pain of release goes to the very core of our being. Yet throughout, another energy remains close by, allowing but comforting, never interfering but providing strength. It is time to honour our true magnificence; the Light beckons us to come home.

The lessons you have chosen are refining and purifying you to accept your rightful place in the universe.

MY EXPERIENCE OF FORGIVENESS

My father was an alcoholic as a very young man and carried within him a lot of pain and anger. Unfortunately he carried it within him until his death at 86 years of age, a terribly long time. The effect of alcoholic parents is well known and rather than repeat all the details, let me just say that I had never forgiven him. I had forgiven him on an intellectual level but in my heart I had not. It seems a small point but our minds tell us one thing, but our hearts know better.

During those early healing times it became my habit to stand and allow spirit guides to work with my body, teaching me to tune into them and to mentally and physically anticipate what part of the body I should attend to next. This exercise was done alone and helped physical and mental channels to open for a more efficient working partnership.

After a clairvoyant friend mentioned that my father was around me quite a lot, I became alerted by the spirit guides that he was there during a practice session. I felt this to be unusual as he had died barely two years before. Why was he around so much? My learning had taught me that he possibly needed to be helped on another level.

With prompting from my guides, I finally realised that he needed my forgiveness before he could move on. This shocked me. Had I been responsible for his staying back, earth bound? What happened next will be with me forever.

The spirit guides brought him to me and because my sense of psychic touch had developed, I could feel his energy field moving closer to me. I cannot describe to you the emotional sensations that began to move inside me and then to surface. Unable to be held in check, my emotional dam wall cracked and my feelings flooded out demanding expression. Tears of release, so painful but so sweet.

My arms were lifted from my side to embrace my father, as I had never done in my 54 years. My pain of withheld love expressed itself. The sobbing slowly abated, as did the pain in my throat as all the unsaid words were released. To feel my father in my arms as he really was moved me deeply. I feel it was a gift of Grace. To have faith is one thing, to know and experience is another. At that moment I knew death to be a fraud. Life is eternal.

Next I was asked to pray for my father. This I did with so much passion and love. During this prayer a ball of golden light surrounded my father; he was sent into the Light to begin his journey once more in Spirit.

He was released from the lower astral plane with love. Love was something he had needed from me all his life. All was not done yet. As my communication was still rough, the whole interaction had taken nearly two hours. Soon, I understood that I needed to pray for myself.

My prayer was for forgiveness, filled with emotion still flowing from the experience with my father. As I prayed I became lighter, understanding that my burdens were being lifted. Our emotional burdens will be taken from us piece by piece over time, this one was large and heavy and now it was going. The forgiveness I asked for was for dishonouring myself. As divine beings we dishonour ourselves with our lack of forgiveness as much as the person we need to forgive.

The next day while driving to work, I realised that a knot in my stomach that had been with me all my life had gone. My thoughts turned to my father. I felt a smile on my face and a feeling of love for him in my heart for the first time; a warm love, with a depth of feeling I had not experienced before. How wonderful it is to know that it is never too late to forgive.

Knowing where he was made me feel warm inside. The fear of death had been washed away. As I was to find out later in my healing experiences, "Those who work in the Light have no fear". There is a loving divine energy with infinite patience.

When all accounts are settled, you can begin to live.

Because you are neither the slave of time, nor caught in the constant cry of the heart. You can begin to thrive … not just survive … thrive.

Guru Maharaji.

TRUE FORGIVENESS

Once true forgiveness is completed with one soul, it is accomplished for every soul. Forgiveness will reside in your heart from that day forward. When this lesson is fully learned, we need not keep repeating it. The lesson of forgiveness shows us that love is the only experience we ever want in our hearts forever.

The stain on ourselves is so damaging when we do not practise forgiveness and an awakening eventually occurs through seeing our own incredibly thoughtless acts. As we see our ignorance, we see our path to *enlightenment*.

The horror of our actions repels us so that we are eventually led to seek forgiveness for ourselves. In this act of seeking, we see the need to forgive others, no matter what they may have done and the freedom forgiveness brings us is complete.

TWO TYPES OF FORGIVENESS

There are two types of forgiveness. The first, and easier one, is by the intellectual path. The ego is in control here. We say, with a grandiose wave of the arm, "Oh I have forgiven them for that", making light of the whole subject, busy convincing ourselves and others that this is true.

The second path is through the heart and we become defenceless. All the emotional pain from the heart and body is released in the most wonderful act of cleansing. This path takes courage and honesty with yourself; every cell in your body holds the fear. It is powerful, painful and wonderful all at once; an experience you will always remember and cherish. because you have just been reborn. You have new eyes through which to see the world. Strange but beautiful things occur when you release through the heart, allow the fear to be there and drop your ego's defences. You can do it.

When you forgive, you do it with your whole being. You become a child again without defences. Any form of defence will stop forgiveness.

THE RIVER OF LOVE THAT FLOWS THROUGH US IS THE INNER PATHWAY

We may or may not enlighten ourselves by many means; by standing on our head, by saying prayers continuously, by focusing on an object for the purpose of stilling the mind or by any spiritual practice that disciplines our bodies. *When we forgive others and ourselves, we have opened the floodgate so that the river of life can flow through us and change our consciousness.*

When a lack of forgiveness arises or anger pops up, we immediately replace it with love, realising that we do not want to tread that path again.

It is essential that all stains from not forgiving are washed away. To truly love another soul this must happen. If you have not forgiven your father or mother, your ex partner or anyone that you perceive has wronged you, then you can never fully experience love, or give love fully to another. Once Universal Love flows through our hearts, the cleansing begins, and it's not always easy.

Do not be stressed that you have not forgiven. As love changes your mind, it is inevitable that forgiveness will come. True forgiveness comes in its own time. When love opens the door, we constantly correct and refine our behaviour, gradually bringing ourselves to a state of Love where fear cannot exist.

If you hold a strong desire to become the Loving Soul that you know you are, it will happen.

LESSON 3

Self-Forgiveness
Key To Joy And Happiness

LOOKING AT YOUR CHILDHOOD

During the first seven years of life, the die is cast. Not an original statement, but true. I would strongly recommend that if you had a traumatic childhood, as many of us have had, have a therapist help you through your inner exploration.

When intense past pain surfaces, skilled assistance is necessary for you to clear it properly. If you have had a fairly average childhood with the usual mother and father issues, I recommend you purchase John Bradshaw's The Homecoming or another suitable publication of his, as his workbook and knowledge is invaluable.

In our formative years the seeds are sown for our future. Everything that has happened to you resides in your cellular memory. If it is intense enough you may have body pain in the organs or muscle structure, with corresponding deviations in your posture. During our regression into earlier memories there will be a reaction from the body as releases occur.

Forgotten emotions surface for release. Sometimes old pains resurface that we thought had healed or had just gone away. Smells, feelings, sounds and visions are not uncommon as the body releases. The journey backward in time is a pathway that is necessary for healing of self. Fear is always present, but it is here we begin to learn about facing our fears.

A WORD OF CAUTION

While I have had a lot of experience assisting others, and working through my own abuse, I would caution anyone who has suffered sexual abuse not to attempt self-healing without a therapist. Any serious abuse or trauma requires one-on-one counselling until the person is ready for self-healing. If you suspect some deep underlying issues, see a therapist.

The average person will find their journey of rediscovery into the past emotional. Sometimes you will get angry or sad, and experience a whole range of emotions while you investigate and release. The past also has its share of joy and warm fuzzy memories. Indulge yourself in these and feel them before releasing them with love, as you will with all memories. Remind yourself that enlightenment comes through letting go, and that is letting go of everything and allowing yourself to be who you are. You are letting go of withheld energies associated with the experience, not the memories themselves. You could not do that anyway. This subject is dealt with in more depth in Lesson 6.

WHY IT IS NECESSARY TO LOOK AT THE PAST

In one sense, it does not matter what we have done in the past, but why we did it. You will discover the why when you look back in your life. Once the why has been objectively looked at, you will set yourself free in the present. The reward far outweighs the effort. Guilt diminishes rapidly as you look with new eyes at your actions without harsh judgement. I say harsh judgement because I know you will still judge yourself as I judge myself at times, far too harshly. We take every opportunity to beat up on ourselves. Never mind, we will improve with practice!

LESSONS LEARNED CAN BE LET GO OF

During the exercise of seeing why you do things, deeper insights occur. Along with that comes the understanding that, at last, guilt can be dealt with. Letting go of an experience that holds guilt for you is easier when you fully understand your actions and see their origin.

MAKING PEACE WITH THE PAST THROUGH CURRENT ACTIONS

Our new understanding brings with it the opportunity to rectify the past. Some New Age and spiritual writers and teachers say the past is the past and nothing can be done about it. I do not agree. What we have done in the past can be undone in the present. And it can be undone with other players if the original players are no longer available.

For example, if our past behaviour was arrogant and selfish towards our partner, then we looked at our upbringing and earlier life experiences, we see why. The chance is there for us to modify our behaviour in the present to atone for our past actions.

If we do not do this, we demonstrate a lack of spiritual growth and will reap our future accordingly.

To have an opportunity to get it right is a precious gift. To have the chance to put away the arrogant behaviour and selfishness by serving and loving another changes the past. The lesson is learnt. And it must be learnt through the heart with love and devotion, not intellectual actions taken with clenched teeth. A lesson is really an opportunity offered by Divine Grace; a gift of love so great that there is no time limit placed upon us and no judgement. The energies of the learnt lesson go back to the beginning of time. The cellular memory is changed and the sins of the parents are not passed on to the children. As we go through our past lessons in the present, all is revealed, and insights occur to enlighten us, and then it is done. You are free!

WITH UNDERSTANDING COMES SELF-FORGIVENESS

It is all about understanding one's self and actions. On achieving this, guilt will go. The play of life, and all the players, can bring down the curtain on the final act as guilt leaves the centre stage that it has occupied for so long. Love and forgiveness is the light that takes us back into life with new eyes. To finally forgive yourself for the past is freeing. You and I deserve to live a full life, not just survive.

SELF-FORGIVENESS: THE STRUGGLE WITH THE EGO

Here we enter an arena of battle where our ego presents us with a two-edged sword.

1. You are told by the ego that, perhaps, you have been too hard with your self-judgement, that really you are a nice person undeserving of all this self-criticism. This is true, but the ego twists and turns and uses elements of truth to hold you in fear. Then the ego continues with; "when you think about it, self-forgiveness is not really necessary. Everybody does these things, so give yourself a break, you don't need to get into self-forgiveness. After all, they did it to you, or what you did is not much different to anyone else. You, in many ways, are the true victim."

2. The other edge of the sword is; "you are so unworthy, and who on earth do you think you are that you could ever forgive yourself for the things you have done in your life? You're sick, you are heartless and cruel. Forgiving yourself is impossible. You do not deserve for-

giveness." After beating ourselves up for a while, we swing back into number 1, which affords us a measure of peace, then back into the cycle to number 2. This tortuous journey continues until we give up, let go, drop our defences and begin to find our own Truth within. This cycle of self-flagellation is the province of fear not love. Be diligent and see the struggle, be strong and be the Master that you already are. Seek assistance.

SPIRITUAL REBIRTH

From here, there is only one place left that will guide us to the Truth, and that is the love in our heart. Expressing Love is doing what we are here for. That Love takes us gently into seeing what we need to do so that we can forgive ourselves. Our inner self is like a child, new born and tender, needing Truth, gentleness and a Love that is willing to forgive anything.

Bringing our attention into our centre of Love locks out the negative and contradictory thoughts that pull us back and forth, never giving us peace, always promising but never delivering. To empower this belief that we are loving divine beings will bring great karmic results. Your self- worth is far greater than you could ever imagine. Guilt will hold a child of Light back from self-realisation; this goes against the Divine plan for you. stop it.

The rebirth of self is imminent, be gentle with yourself. The Inner Light is finding expression. The new child is fragile and innocent. Be kind and tolerant with it, it is you, the Universe's gift to the rest of the world. You reflect the power and glory of Creation. You have a right to be here in all your glory. You stand ready to be reborn, let the river of Love within take you home. No more guilt and no more pain.

LESSON 4

Self-Love
A Most Necessary Action

BEING WITH YOURSELF

The busyness of life is self-created for a number of reasons, but mainly because to sit still and be with ourselves is daunting. Filling up our lives is easier. By doing this, we numb the pain of being lost. Have you ever sat down and started to fidget? Looked for something to do? That is a common symptom of avoidance. An avoidance of being still. For many people, being still is too much to ask. Being busy is fine, provided you know when you need the quiet times and you welcome them. The art of being still is largely lost and needs to be rediscovered.

Start with five minutes (or less if you need to) per day of being with yourself. Sit still and let your mind be still, or quieter than normal. You owe it to yourself. Enrol in a meditation class. You need quiet time. Time to be in touch with your inner self is an investment you will not regret. Extend the quiet time until you can sit for 30 minutes or more without feeling fidgety.

Use this time to meditate any way you wish, but generally to honour your being, and get back in touch with yourself and your spiritual needs in life.

LETTING GO OF WHAT YOU ARE NOT

Every experience we judge as being good or bad accumulates in our spiritual body. We carry all these judged experiences with us. When we board the spiritual aircraft, we find that there is a price to pay for this excess baggage; that is, there can be no spiritual advancement until we deal with it. In other words, when the excess baggage is left behind, we can take off on our flight.

I can hear some of you saying, "but I did not judge the good things that happened to me!" Yes you did, you judged them as good. You are judging what you are reading as something you like or dislike. Furthermore, your past experiences colour what you read and this will also affect your judgement. Your understanding will be compatible with your judgement coloured by past experiences, and this will change your experience in the moment.

All our distorted views and beliefs and actions are not us. It is essential for us to rid ourselves of past judgements, to dump this baggage. We do it gradually, piece by piece. With fresh perception we can really understand what is written.

As we begin to love ourselves, we still look at the past with judgements made through the ego's fear. We are not able to love what we perceive as us. Our perception is distorted and full of fear and guilt. To love ourselves, we need to let go of all we are not, and discover the true beauty within.

Many religious institutions reaffirm what our parents may have also told us, that we are not good enough. We were told that, in the eyes of God, we are sinners and unworthy. Fear was used to increase attendances at church. These dangerous and negative affirmations are repeated over and over, doing untold damage. Today, we still struggle to see our inherent beauty as children of the Divine because of the seeds of fear and guilt planted within us.

KNOWING YOU ARE NOT THE BODY

Body consciousness is an enemy of self-love. It must be rooted out and discarded. The focus on body worship has caused many beautiful souls to lose their way. Many gifted people have robbed the world of their presence through an unhealthy focus on the body. Our vehicle has a divine purpose; that is, to experience a three-dimensional world, learn our lessons and attain enlightenment in a physical body.

To have a physical body is an extraordinary gift of love. In this body we can experience all the physical and spiritual gifts at the same time. You had to earn the chance to become master of your physical and spiritual body. To become a master you require a body. In this body we have unlimited opportunities for experiences that reverberate from the spiritual realms into the physical and back into the spiritual. Along with emotions, thoughts, desires, words, actions, the body is only a vehicle which makes the depth of the experiences possible.

Understanding that our body reacts to every thought we have, we must take care. We need to be balanced in our treatment of our bodies; no excessive behaviour, moderation in food and drink, sensible care and maintenance and, most importantly, balanced loving thoughts about our body.

If, for some reason, you do not honour your body and wish to leave it, consider this. The third dimensional world affords us the luxury of time delay. In this life when we think, say or do, we wait for a result, whatever that may be, Within this delay period, we also have time to rectify mistakes.

In spiritual realms there is no delay. The moment the thought has been formed in the mind, it is manifested. Another point to consider is that our emotions are approximately ten times more overwhelming in spirit. Demons from our mind appear immediately in front of us. Feel like sticking around a little longer? I think so. So love yourself in this life. Honour your body as a part of the total experience.

Your existence in consciousness is not dependent on the body, the body is a gift of love for your experience and learning on this plane. Do not focus all your attention on the body because it is very temporary in its present form.

SENSING YOUR DIVINITY

Focus on your divinity, discard the negative suggestions of the past. Every day, empower a growing feeling within you of beauty, peace and love. Know that you were created out of love and you are loved unconditionally. Keep on allowing your deep inner knowing of your divinity to grow stronger every day. The Divine within you is your source of everything. Everything you need comes from there, focus on it and empower your life. Your quiet times are valuable for this practice.

HONOURING YOU

Looking through the eyes of guilt will ensure that we never honour ourselves. But we may pursue the inner Spirit and in doing so see the Light within us. When we honour ourselves as an expression of Pure Consciousness and Love, and radiate that love in all its forms, we honour the Divine within us. And we can become one with It. The next time you feel like dishonouring your being, remember who you really are.

HUMILITY AND ACCEPTANCE

Life is a gift, given without conditions. As ego-based entities, we only have fear. As an extension of the inner Divine, we have it all. No request is left unfulfilled on our journey of learning. We can travel in any desired direction and can do whatever we want. In our learning, we are not judged. We set up our own judgements and, as we see our mistakes, we are merciless with ourselves. We create and keep our own records. Yet through all of this, we are loved in a way we do not understand. A person who has committed the foulest deeds can always come home to the Light. Eventually, through self-learning we find humility and the inner Divine. We understand that we are children of the Universe, loved and cared for on a cyclic journey of self-discovery, eternal and beautiful. We see a divine plan so perfect that we are humbled by its breadth and scope as it unfolds before us.

LISTING YOUR GIFTS TO THE WORLD

There is a plan for you. This plan will be revealed to you when you are ready for it. Your uniqueness is reflected in your life's plan. In the expression of your life there are gifts that you will present to the world and only you can bring them to fruition. Only fear prevents the plan from manifesting.

Your role does not have to be centre-stage to do what you need to do. A mother's love for her child is a gift so great that the world is dependent on each child receiving this. Without this love the world will crumble into darkness. The cornerstone of the world is the feminine energy, the nurturing and loving energy that puts in place the foundation for light to shine on this planet. A mature man who cannot display a balanced male/female energy finds life lacking and misses out on many beautiful moments.

To receive this love that they secretly crave, men strut the world's stage like peacocks in the hope of attracting it to them. Women who have not received feminine love and nurturing tend to feel worthless and withdraw.

A father builds on feminine energy by bringing to the child a masculine energy of doing, constructing and building. In balance, both energies produce a being who can achieve great things. When out of balance, a person can either be too weak and fearful to express their life's work and may show displays of anger or become overpowering and demanding with excess male energy. Some high achievers, in a bid for love, use excess male energy to overcome perceived opposition in order to achieve their goals. The story of Adolf Hitler's childhood is horrific, where he received no mother's love at all. The results are well-known. It is well-documented that he was a lonely and isolated person. The fear within him drove him relentlessly to achieve what he perceived as greatness, at any cost.

Your special gift to the world will be found in a foundation of love, whether you are male or female. You are not starved of the love that really counts, it flows from the Inner Divinity. Let it shine.

SEEING THE BEAUTY IN EVERY SOUL

As we look back over our lives thus far, the focus of the ego goes to things we have said and done that are fear-based, raising guilt into our consciousness. This automatic reflex does nothing to enhance our lives on any level. We have become so accustomed to de-valuing ourselves that rarely do we consider our actions that have enhanced our own and others' lives. There is a need to bring balance to where guilt controls us. Self-love can set us free from this most terrible of masters. But first guilt must go.

Blame placed upon our parents or others for our upbringing can be of short-term value only, until spiritual responsibility has been reached. In the clear light of self-responsibility we must embrace our darkness and deal with it. Self-love is not about loving our thoughts, words or actions but looking inside and feeling with our hearts, ours and others' inherent beauty as Divine Beings growing together, creating lessons, learning and forgiving.

After true forgiveness has been reached, we extend love, compassion and tolerance to our brothers and sisters. When our brothers and sisters behave badly it may become necessary to put some physical distance between us and them, but we can still recognise their Divinity from seeing our own. You are not being asked to put up with fear-based activities that are anti-social; you do not have to love someone's bad behaviour.

You may recognise the profound feelings you have that at times run so deep into the river of that life that tears well up and your heart sings. There are no words, just love. You can only go there when you have put down your excess luggage (let go sufficiently) and your mind is quiet so that your awareness can see who you are and experience it. You have experienced your true self and this self you can love.

The more you meditate on your inner beauty the more you will empower it to manifest in your life. Be persistent, keep knocking on the door. You are not the thoughts and emotions that appear from nowhere and run you around in circles or the words you spoke and would dearly like to take back. Nor are you the actions that have resulted from these seemingly uncontrollable states you find yourself in. You are none of these things. The person you believe you are is a direct extension of the mental state you hold and that changes as often as the weather. So you cannot be that. We are so changeable because we reflect our momentarily held mental state, like emotional chameleons, changing in and out of our differing mental states and producing a mask to go with it. To be happy one day and sad another day is exhausting. A perfect Universal Energy could not create such imperfection as reflections of its Divine Self.

What you really are is Pure Consciousness and Knowledge born of Love.

If we were shown how magical we are, we probably would have great difficulty believing it, and start creating more problems for ourselves. So perhaps a gradual awakening is best. The slow awakening to our majestic beauty and multi-dimensional being comes in small easily digestible bites, as and when we grow enough to cope. As we discard what we are not and embrace who we are, loving ourselves becomes easy.

ILLUSION OF SEPARATION

Separation from our Light is a delusion held by us since the beginning of free will, when we chose fear. The manufactured ego replaced the trust that the Divine would care for us. Knowing that all the powers of creation were our birthright we still let go of the sure knowledge that our lives could flow unhindered in the Divine Plan for us and exchanged that beauty for an ego that shows us no mercy. Happiness and fulfilment are our Divine right. Instead we fear, and so our life of dreaming and apparent separation from our Light began. There has never been a separation, we only believe this is so. The mighty lion of life has accepted the role of scavenger and lives off the scraps far below the place set for him at the table of Creation. From the pinnacle of creation, it is lost and bedraggled, suffering delusion by its own hand. While Divine Energy sees only perfection, we see a worthless creature unfit for anything.

The way out of this bad dream is to change our mind and our reality must change. We wallow in fear and guilt perpetuating our own nightmare. Inside each one of us burns the Light of the Divine. When we see this within us and let our ego be stilled, the Truth inside us will be freed.

SELF-INFLICTED PUNISHMENT

It is now time for us to let go of our bad dream by replacing it with love. How can the Creator of perfection be expected to share in our dream of imperfection? What an insane idea. The Truth would never support such an outrageous concept. There is no judgement from Divine consciousness. We support the proposition that the Divine loves us, and then create our own pain and lessons, and then say we are being punished. No one could ever be as cruel to us as we can be to ourselves. No one could ever judge a Divine Being as worthless except us. No one could ever put us through lifetimes of torture except us. We persist in the belief that we are totally unworthy and fit only for endless cycles of reincarnation with endless suffering. What type of crazy thinking perpetuates this cycle? We lash out at others, denigrate ourselves, hold fear about everything in life and we dishonour our Being terribly.

LOVE, OUR NATURAL STATE

We were created in the vibration of love, to experience our individual consciousness within the mind of Divinity, which is Love and Light beyond our current limited concepts. Yet in fleeting moments of joy and ecstasy we have these very experiences. Mostly we believe that someone else was the cause of our inner experience and if they go away, we will lose that very precious gift. Once again our thinking is fearful. How can an inner experience of love be dependent on an outer set of conditions, even if you do love that person? Love exists within us and can be experienced as joy and happiness continuously. It is only our fear (feeling of lack or need) that blocks the experience, and periodically someone comes into our life and sets it off and we once again believe that we need that person exclusively for our happiness. Even when the other person is not in our presence, we feel love and immediately identify the feeling with that person. The love we feel for that person is very real, so is the inner experience of self. To share the experience of love with another is a gift of such beauty. We have the inner experience and then radiate it to the other, what a wonderful and special gift. However, sometimes when they are with us judgement creeps in and we lose the feeling of love. What is happening here is that we are having an internal experience that has no interdependence on what is happening on the outside. We only believe that this is so. It is our state of mind that dictates what we experience, not what is occurring outside us.

What is happening is our inner experience of love is intensifying or decreasing, and we directly attribute it to the other person. Within the True Love experience there is a sharing of freedom and love for the other soul for who they are, a sharing of the Divinity and uniqueness, while acknowledging their total freedom to experience their own lessons. *Unless we learn to love a soul for who they are, we shall always be loving them for our own selves, and manipulating them to fit into our needs.* A selfish love like this is doomed and certain to create attachment and dependency and eventually pain, because sooner or later they will go away, one way or the other.

If external conditions created our happiness then everyone would be happy for the same reasons and we know this is not true. Total joy and happiness can be had anywhere at any time regardless of external conditions. We can be blissed out in a traffic jam or in meditation. Our state of mind creates our reality and therefore our internal experience of life. Everything is internalised, you experience everything on the inside. If you empower external events, then that is what decides if and when you will experience love and joy in your life, a very shaky basis for happiness. However, souls come together to experience the Love that they are. By igniting the flame within, we may experience the beauty within each other and, in doing so, recognise ourselves.

LOVE IN THE BODY

Currently most of us carry more fear in our bodies than love. We feel as much love for our bodies as we would a motor vehicle and in some cases we love the car more. When our body aches for attention, we ignore it. When our car rattles, we worry about it until it's fixed. If we begin to love and care for our bodies as much as our material possessions, we'd progress rapidly. Every single cell responds to our thoughts. What are you thinking about? And what are you hanging on to?

When every cell in our body vibrates to the love frequency, our bodies will once again feel like a loving cloak that envelopes us like a satin gown of pure energy, moving easily in coordination with our loving thoughts. There can be no possibility of us embracing a consciousness of unconditional love until we have cleansed ourselves sufficiently so that it can take place. The vibration of unconditional love is so high that while experiencing it, we say, "stop," we cannot handle it.

A quote attributed to Sathya Sai Baba says, " I cannot fill you up until I squeeze you dry". You can do the squeezing by doing the work. We cannot have what we want without a change of mind. The purification process must be gone through. Thoughts, words and actions are cleansed so that we can sustain a change of consciousness. Then our body will vibrate in a frequency that harmonises with our state of consciousness.

THE REFLECTION OF TWIN FLAMES

Understanding that love is you, your own personal experience, and honouring the other soul and acknowledging their freedom and uniqueness enhances experience and deepens the love we have for each other. These twin flames reflect and enhance one's inner experience. Life and love are eternal, there is no end to either. Rejoice in the knowledge that once two hearts are joined, they are forever linked. The experience remains forever with both souls. When forgiveness is completed in a separation, only the love and the lesson remain and the soul's experience is expanded. Any feelings that remain after separation other than love, are wasteful and limiting to the growth of the soul and cause us to reincarnate.

LESSON 5

Letting Go
The Journey For Your Life

WHAT IS LETTING GO?

Letting go can be the most terrifying experience that we can go through. Letting go means having no support mechanism for our ego. By letting go, we trust that everything is going to work out in our best interest, even when an experience screams out to us to hang on. Life is not a series of unrelated cosmic accidents, our life flows from within. The holes we fall into were dug by us at an earlier time, when we were unaware of it. Our thoughts, words and actions were creating our future experiences while we were thinking, speaking, and acting on them. We created our present experience.

WHAT IS THERE TO LET GO OF?

Let go of all judgement, let go of trying to solve other people's problems, of manipulating and controlling the lives of people close to you, and of forcing your life to go in directions that your mind tells you it must go. Let go of the need to arrange your physical world so that you can be happy. Stop reacting to thoughts and emotions with fear. Fear alone is responsible for us holding on to what we term as "our life".

The biggest package to let go is of the concepts we hold about everything. Our concepts about the way things are, and our expectations of them. We base our happiness on an expected outcome without real knowledge or understanding of what is the best result for everyone.

FEAR OF LETTING GO

To let go is to let go of our fear. Fear breeds anger, intolerance, greed, arrogance, selfishness, egotistical behaviour, self-centredness and a host of other destructive traits. We don't want these traits in our life because the behaviour that springs from them separates us from our Light. These fearful behaviour patterns dishonour our Self and the other person and this hurts us greatly. When fear takes hold, we lash out in our defence even more strongly to hide our pain and dishonouring of Self. Courage and strength are needed to let go and you can do it. You can take away pieces of who you are not and let them go gradually, you don't have to do it in one go. You're in charge.

WE NEED TO BE A VICTIM FIRST

In the early stages of personal growth, we are not open to other ideas or concepts. We are generally resistant to ideas such as "why did you bring this into your life?" Or friends who say, "You will be fine, stop worrying about it." We find it infuriating, as if they don't care or really understand the way we feel. Chronic body pain manifests, a part of us that is screaming out for attention. Pain, frustration and anger are common. "People just don't understand what I am going through" is a common remark. We visit this victim stage regularly.

We become totally absorbed in our misery and resist anyone who tries to shake us out of it. We want sympathy, not helpful suggestions. We dump the blame on others for our pain and suffering. "No matter what I do or how I organise my life someone always screws it up," we say. The tighter we hang on the greater the pain. The more we try to organise others' lives, the greater the frustration from unfulfilled expectations. Do you think Divine Consciousness is trying to tell us something?

GIVING UP AND LETTING GO

Letting go conjures up images of lack of control, being lost, left behind, loneliness, and perhaps financial ruin. This free fall state appears to offer nothing but pure fear and disaster. The ego has always instructed us that striving and achievement is everything, that letting go will result in a fall with devastating results. No responsible human being does that sort of thing. So we hang on, white knuckled and teeth clenched, in order to appear normal, while we smile through frozen faces and staring eyes to make others feel comfortable as we conform to their expectations. This insanity is perpetuated until we just let go.

THE LETTING GO EXPERIENCE

Sooner or later we become so tired of hanging on to our misery that we simply give up. Hanging on takes so much energy, we become very tired propping up the image we wish to portray, while simultaneously suppressing our emotions. The load gets too heavy to carry. Sooner or later, we must put our burden down. Asking around, we find offers come to us from varied sources of help. We have opened the door.

The letting go becomes a free fall experience like the trust exercise of falling backwards into another's waiting arms. There is fear and total lack of control, and then the helpful and safe hands of support as we land dispels our fear. We experience this many times on our healing journey as our ego struggles for control through fear. As we let go, the fear and stress of hanging on subside, the pain and misery abate and we see we are not alone. There is an immediate improvement in outlook.

AN EXAMPLE

Some years ago, I decided to let go. I left to travel around Australia in a 20-year-old car with a tent, and enough money to reach my first destination. For the next two years I travelled continuously, giving workshops and living in my tent. At 54 years of age the experience was filled with fear. As I let go, my life became magical. So can yours, and you don't have to live in a tent.

WHY HANG ON?

Hanging on causes us so much pain and disappointment, you would think we would be anxious to let go. Unable to comprehend the relief of letting go, we let years block our path to freedom. All this, to satisfy our ego.

We push our children to perform and excel, we insist that our partners walk, talk and act in ways to please us, to please our ego. We reap the consequences of the expectations we put on others, our partners and children. We expect them to act, speak and think the way we want, for our own sakes. To really love them, we must accept everything they say and do as necessary for them and honour their pathway home, as we expect them to honour ours.

The greatest gift we can give our partners is to cut them free of our expectations. In this single action we free ourselves to experience happiness in our relationships.

We generally try to change things around us, to improve them. If we see a forest, we believe that a car park would be more useful. We then believe we should grow trees on the car park, forgetting that there were trees there in the first place. After we get our family under control, we start on our older and wiser parents telling them how to live out the rest of their lives. By the time we move on to our friends' behaviour, our children have rebelled, our partner has left us and our world starts to wobble.

Stand by for the stress, pain, nervous breakdowns, physical illnesses and all the other symptoms that hanging on and perceived failure brings. We blame everyone else for our unhappiness, when all we need to do is let go.

REACTIONS TO LETTING GO

When we eventually let go, sometimes all hell breaks loose. We become sicker than ever before. Deeply hidden issues surface like dragons from the past, threatening to eat us alive. Our "normal" life activities are turned on their heads and feelings of panic spread through us, telling us we should have left well alone. Friends judge us and walk out of our lives. Guilt raises its head and blames you for upsetting and destroying others' lives around you.

The day-to-day comfort zone has been shattered and the winds of change are blowing. The winds blow into corners that have not seen light for many lifetimes, and the pain can be almost unbearable. Our greatest fears are unfounded as we let go to the Light. Hanging on causes our distress, freedom is already ours, and we just need to let it be.

The Universe is shifting to meet your newly embraced reality. We still have the same body, the same Soul, but our thinking has changed, and, therefore, so has our reality. The Universe must accommodate us with every change of mind. That is Universal Law.

THE RIVER OF LIFE

During all the crazy activities that we think are essential to our happiness, we block the flow of life from our Divine centre.

Our future experiences vibrate to the confusion that we create by hanging on now. We do not allow what is best for us to come into our lives. By continuing to create confusing karma with our minds, we ensure our future will be the same.

There is a Divine Energy that flows from within, this is the river of life that flows from our heart. The river is gold and silver, pure and radiant, a light vibration of the highest frequency. This light is the Divine light, the highest possible vibration that we can radiate on this plane of existence. When this river of life flows uninterrupted, your life becomes perfect and in harmony with creation's intention for you.

Letting go means plunging into this flow without thoughts of fear and trusting that lifetimes of fear will be reversed and perfection manifested in your life. This happens to Creation's timing. First, we deal with the self-made negativity that already exists in our lives before we can feel the force of the Divine. Letting go has to happen so that the Divine can come in. Depending on our past experiences and reactions to situations, we may have created such beautiful karma that life is a continuous blissful state. Then again, it may not be so.

NOT RESISTING

Letting go is acknowledging that there is a greater power that flows through us, that has our best interest at heart. Without any effort on our part, we can let go to this power and just be. By not resisting, we can let our life flow like a river from our hearts, making room in our life for everything that needs to be there and allowing other things to pass by and move on. The joy of life is in standing still and allowing. We discover that peace comes in when we cease to struggle. When you know you are in a dream, everything can be released.

LESSON 6

Defence
The Illusion Of The Ego

ON THE BRIDGE

We now have a foot in two camps. We have begun to let go, but we are still hanging on. We are standing on the bridge between two realities. In our hearts we know that we need to let go completely but our fear of continuing the free fall stops us. We call it a rest stop, to look around and take stock. In fact, it is just a ploy of the ego to maintain subtle control. The ledge we have grabbed onto cannot sustain us for long. Once we have taken a step on the path, we cannot withdraw, it is impossible to back track. We have reached a point of spiritual awakening and responsibility, we cannot revert back to ignorance. Everything is in the letting go, there is no need to stop. Stopping gives us a false sense of control over our life and a false security. The ego presents us with fear of the unknown to make us hang on once again. Control is a fear-based ego activity. Avoidance is on the agenda again, if only temporarily.

MANIPULATION AND CONTROL

When we manipulate and control our lives, judgement also creeps in. We are back into our karmic filters and the truth is coloured. Free falling is empowering because you override the ego and reclaim your power, letting go to the Divine within, rejecting other people's egos and demands and allowing your Divinity to shine.

It takes courage, but soon becomes a natural experience; you begin to honour yourself for who you are. Compromise is not a word you will listen to. You are either in free fall or not, there is no half way.

> Without defences you become a light which heaven gratefully acknowledges to be it's own. And it will lead you on its ways appointed for your happiness according to the ancient plan, begun when time was born. Your followers will join their light with yours, and it will be increased until the world is lighted up with joy. And gladly will our sisters and brothers lay aside their cumbersome *defences, which availed them nothing and could only terrify.*
>
> *– From 'A Course in Miracles'*

As other people try to intimidate or stifle your Divinity you reply with love and tolerance, because you see and understand the karmic play when judgement is put aside. The lesson bought to you is easily understood. There is nothing to prove or defend to anyone, you are who you are.

LOSS IS AN ILLUSION

Nothing can be taken from you, you cannot lose who you are. You are indestructible and eternal. You are a manifestation of Divine Light, an individual consciousness, what is there to struggle with? Only the perceived threat of loss that the ego presents to us can bring us into fear and delusion and defence. When we understand that loss is impossible, we will not keep falling into the same hole over and over again. *We must eventually see the distorted reality that the ego presents to us and once again embrace love unconditionally.*

TWO MANIFESTATIONS OF SELF-EMPOWERMENT

Two things seem to happen simultaneously at this stage of your self-empowerment.

1. *An outpouring of anger (fear of loss) towards you from others close to you.* This fear can be anything from fear of losing your friendship, to genuine concern that you are losing your grip on reality, as you no longer react in ways that they are used to. This fearful reaction does not always happen, sometimes the reaction is positive.

2. *An inflow of divine energy that stabilises and strengthens.* At this time there can be a strong pull in two different directions as the ego works with fear and your True being works with love. The sensation is like having a long lost friend beside you, giving you the words to speak and the wisdom of the ages from which to draw inspiration. A deep recognition of your Divinity begins to filter into your consciousness. The transformation has begun on a conscious level.

You are reclaiming your Divinity, your power, and your magnificence. The offspring of fear is anger and attack. Recognise when another soul is becoming fearful and respond accordingly. By reacting with love and tolerance, you empower the inner process that has begin and honour yourself. You also honour the other soul by responding in this way. There is a place for controlled anger, we are not unfeeling creatures, our emotions are there for us to learn to use in a controlled way.

FOCUS ON THE GOD WITHIN

By focusing on the inner Light, you manifest it more and more in your life. Soon nothing can dissuade you from taking back your life and offering it to the part of you that is perfect and true. An inner strength will develop that will amaze you and the most wonderful thing is, that it is you.

SPIRITUAL TESTS

Tests that come our way are not Divine intervention or some hierarchy in spirit testing us. It is our consciousness changing, propelling us into new experiences for our growth. These testing experiences have always existed in our lives, we did not see them for what they were. We can have the same conversation with the same person six months apart and each will be a different experience.

Which reaction from us is the one that recognises the truth? Possibly neither one, possibly both. We can see the futility of trying to bend others to our way of thinking as our own thinking is so volatile and destined to change. We want others to think the way we do so that we feel in control. This is the road to suffering. The roller coaster ride of emotion as we struggle to get others to conform to our concepts of how they should behave is the work of the ego.

DIS-EMPOWERING THE EGO

In the Bible when Satan tempts Jesus with all the kingdoms and riches of the world, Jesus said, "get thee behind me Satan." My interpretation is that this was the voice of his ego. Being a spiritually evolved being, he made that statement and turned away. His ego was completely beaten. Not by confrontation but by empowering spiritual values. As Jesus was one with the Father, the transient nature of the world held no attraction for him. If Jesus and other teachers were tempted throughout their lives by the ego then we must draw the conclusion that the ego is with us throughout this lifetime. How we view the ego and its works does not affect its function, it still controls us the same way.

If a person fights disease by utilising all their powers to struggle against it, they are, in fact, empowering the disease in their life. When people focus on what is wrong with them and how difficult it is to get rid of the problem, they reinforce the illness.

To walk away and focus on spiritual values we hold dear makes us strong. We hear of people diagnosed with life threatening diseases who walk out of the doctor's office and say, "I do not have time for this, there is too much yet to do with my life" and, magically, the disease retreats. The disease has not been confronted but ignored and positive affirmations put to work. There is a change of consciousness where disease cannot exist. Something only has to be done once to prove that it can be done. To beat the ego at its own game is to turn away and empower love.

LESSON 7

Judgement and Actions
The Road To Delusion

JUDGEMENT AND CONSEQUENCES

We are drawn into other people's consequences by giving consent to their actions or by judging their behaviour. The energy field that links us together works on all levels, spiritual and physical. We constantly expend energy for the approval or disapproval of our friends and family. When energy comes to you from another person, the judgement you attach to it ties you to it, regardless of the judgement made.

Without judgement, you remain free. Love, compassion and respecting others' free will keeps you free and independent of others' consequences. Being drawn into other people's issues is our downfall. We can discuss, advise carefully and be there for someone, but judgement is the banana skin we slip on. Our past determines our perception of truth in this moment. Because we have placed judgement on past events and people, we cannot see clearly in the present.

When we judge we are saying that we know the answer to a person's problem. No two people tread the same path. No two people share exactly the same feelings. No two people experience the same reality, so how can we know what is exactly right for another soul? Skilled counsellors carefully guide people to their own solutions and, if they are wise, do not make judgements. I liken others' issues to cobwebs of energy, set to trap similar vibrations and, if we wish, we can become entangled in them. We then make their issues our own and fill our lives with them and leave no time for our selves.

We become physically and emotionally exhausted and unable to take care of ourselves or others. It is wiser to suggest counselling to those we wish to help and then to support them with love, compassion and practical help. We judge so quickly that we barely know when it occurs.

Furthermore, emotion, stimulated by judgement, floods in and we are overwhelmed. Our reaction is decided by past experiences which colour the truth or reality of the situation.

Three things need to be observed:

- First, learn to stop judging, but also be tolerant and understanding of yourself as you learn mastery.
- Second, control your emotions. Do not suppress them but allow them and feel them and let them go just as you would a thought that you no longer desire to have. We do not have to react to our emotions any more than we do our thoughts. We do not deny that we think, so do not deny your emotions.
- Third, the thought had a birthplace. Where did it come from? Look at your past judgements. The thought, the emotion and the judgement possibly had absolutely nothing to do with what is actually happening.The truth cannot be seen through the past, Therefore we are in delusion. The absence of judgement lets us see Truth.

SEEING THE EXPERIENCES WITHOUT JUDGEMENT

Problems begin to accumulate in our bodies as we judge people and events in our life. What we judge as good, another person may judge as unacceptable. Ten people in a room will judge the same event in different ways. You tell me who is right? Letting go of judgement is so difficult, because we are so good at it. Understand your present judgements in the light of past events.

THE KARMIC WEB

Every thought, every word, every action of ours is community property, just like a fish in the ocean where each movement sends vibrations through the sea around it. Our thoughts generate a vibration in our energy field that attract thoughts of a like vibration. Continued negative thinking generates a heavy and depressing atmosphere in our aura and soon repels or attracts people near us. The opposite is also true, of course.

It is interesting to note that beneath our confusion our Inner Light still manages to shine. Others recognise our Light and come to our aid in time of need, ignoring the outer blanket of negativity.

THE EGO'S GAME

Our ego tells us how wonderful we are for saving all these people from themselves and our spiritual development is put on hold. For numerous lifetimes we have involved ourselves in the karmic play of birth, death and others' issues. How long are we going to continue to put off our own spiritual growth? How much longer are we going to play the avoidance game by busily looking after others so that we don't have to look at ourselves? Interaction between people is how we learn, but the lesson needs to be brought back inside and learnt.

Everything that you experience is happening on the inside. everything in life is an internal experience. Life is an inner journey. When are we going to finally realise that we are not consciously enlightened enough to solve everyone else's problems? When do we enlighten ourselves? Will we take notice of the Masters' demonstration of allowing with love and compassion and not interfering? Taking away another person's opportunity to learn makes it harder for them and binds you to them karmicly, so you will continue to experience lessons together.

RELEASING YOURSELF FROM THE GAME

Your love and compassion will do more for your sister and brother than ego-driven rescues, no matter how major they may be.

A hiker leaves the lost and fearful group to find the trail home and refuses to play the game of fear and illusion and of being lost. He strikes out fearlessly, ignoring the cries from the others that they will surely perish if left alone. He finds the way and returns and shows the others the way home. Some have died from fear, but the majority are saved. If he had not had the courage to leave they would have all perished. This person is the real hero. Save yourself first then go back and show your Light to others. This is the ultimate rescue. It takes more courage to show the way than to follow. This does not mean you abandon those who need a helping hand. It is the way you give assistance that matters. Love and compassion are your tools. Each person needs to play out his or her role, learn the lesson and move on, without interference. Don't weave unnecessary karmic webs, become free.

THE KEEPER OF OUR OWN KARMIC RECORDS

Sometimes lessons come to us that appear not to relate to our current state of mind. We may have been positive and loving for some time, working hard to improve, when a lesson comes from the past that we thought we had left behind.

A simple and apparently harmless statement can trigger another lesson. A word reverberates into universal energy and brings to us a situation from the past that we thought we had dealt with. The lesson may come in a form that is not easily recognised. Nothing we need to release is forgotten under karmic law. Everything is written in our records of which we are the keepers. We decide the timing and intensity of lessons through our thoughts, words and actions.

CREATING OUR OWN LESSONS

We write our own karma. We arrange our own learning by the vibration of the thoughts, words and actions we release into the cosmic ocean. Our thoughts in each moment create the next moment and so on. We decide what goes and what stays. Our counsellors in spirit help to modify our behaviour so that we continue to get better.

It's up to us. We are the masters of our own destiny. Nobody does anything to us or for us. For us to receive from Spirit, we must have first have earned it. The most loving non-judgmental law is at our disposal and allows us to learn our lessons in our own time. The infinite patience of Creation sees only perfection in us.

That loving law is the Law of Karma (the law of action). Within this law, we create an intricate web, sensitive to the most subtle vibrations. We reap exactly what we sow in each moment.

The process of growth does not cease with the end of each lifetime and the energy of each new soul attracts its chosen lessons. Whether the lesson comes in childhood or adulthood, the soul learns and moves on.

We bring with us into life vibrational records, belief systems, likes and dislikes. We bring all the influences that we have accumulated in previous lives. We begin the next incarnation with these burdens.

A child of six months has developed belief systems in place, though they have not fully become part of their consciousness. Then parental influences and life experiences modify and mould them, sometimes in a positive way but often negatively. We have all marvelled at how a young child has likes and dislikes and is individual in characteristics foreign to the parents. We see a child, but, in fact, they may be souls far older than us and wiser.

If parents have no solid belief system to live by this leads to confusion in future karma. The future will be the result of the beliefs. Our beliefs, thinking and focus create vibrations that in turn create our reality (future karma). The universe can only deliver what we ask for through the vehicle of our thoughts, words and actions. The soul's journey is in line with the need to learn and grow. Lessons chosen are the right and choice of the incarnating soul.

We may continually ask "why did this happen?" but we may never know, for the journey is sacred to each soul and we must honour and accept each soul's path. It is the lesson that is important not the form it takes. Why we do things is what matters. All this relates to the vibrational history we bring with us. Love and compassion are there for us to express to the suffering soul so that we may ease the pain and lighten the load. That is also part of experience and learning. I make no apology for answers that come from thousands of years of spiritual teachings.

Belief systems create karma. Bad karma, good karma, there is only karma or results of action. Blame and guilt intimates that there has to be a victim, but this comes from fear.

We will not see truth until we stop judging others. You are expressing fear when you step into judgement. If you say you are guilty of being in the wrong place, guilty of being too sensitive, then you are expressing fear. There is no fear without judgement. It becomes an experience in your reality, nobody else's. Guilt and blame must be dispensed with.

Truth is relevant to your reality and experience. I cannot completely experience your truth nor you mine. But both are real and true and are to be honoured without judgement. The ultimate truth is that all is Divine Consciousness. When we believe this wholly, fear subsides and our reality will shift from fear to love.

Projection of blame and guilt onto others and turning away from their misfortunes is born of fear. This is when you need the most help. But we, each of us, is affected by the other's misfortune. We are not separate. Every unselfish act adds to the positive vibrations of the group soul.

Spiritual growth is achieved through the many different opportunities to learn which are disguised as life experiences. At the time we may wonder why. If we are non-judgemental of the situation and loving and compassionate and do our utmost to help all souls who ask, we live in the greatest power of protection we can receive.

LESSON 8

Relating To Others
Mirror Mirror On The Wall

LEARNING THROUGH RELATIONSHIPS

Insights come from the heart. Perhaps the intellect can be a vehicle for enlightenment, but for me and millions of others the pathway from the heart is the most healing and beautiful way.

Relationships with friends and family are all learning opportunities. They come in many forms and can take up hours of intellectual discussion. But there is only one lesson to learn – to give service unselfishly to your partner or friend and others that may knock on your door.

Enlightened individuals like Mother Teresa demonstrate true selflessness to us. Most of us would say this level of service is unattainable for us and not in our present learning.

BEING MINDFUL

Awareness of our thoughts, words and actions can overwhelm us and we may give up. But, as we progress, mindfulness is vital and attainable.

Your ego will always be prepared to remind you of all

the things you need to do for yourself. But truthfully, how many things do we really need to do?

How much joy and satisfaction do we draw from them? Serving others is a way of learning some very hard lessons. Service brings out our lack of capacity to give.

Partnerships give us many opportunities to put aside our own personal desires by giving with love to our partner. Serving our partner is not meant to be a servile, mindless duty, but a giving of love through the highest channel available to us, no matter how menial the task. Remember to practise balance in all things.

AN EXAMPLE OF NOT BEING MINDFUL

One evening I was discussing a response to a letter I had received with my wife Ruth. Ruth agreed to help me with the reply and worked hard on it. I made the mindless comment, "Well, I may as well rewrite the whole letter," with no forethought and was hurtful towards someone who gave me their love and assistance. Though we say and do things without any intention to hurt, mindless acts can hurt others.

SELFLESSNESS

As we serve with love, and learn selflessness, we approach the Divine through the pathway of love and forgiveness. Subtle feelings in our heart sing of a new consciousness. A new age of light dawns where the unifying power of love washes away the darkness of the past. The small I (the ego) begins to lose its grip over the experience of the soul forever. Freedom is within reach. Personal needs are lovingly and willingly replaced by the needs of others. As the ego loses its hold, there is a feeling of an expanded consciousness where your needs are met through service to others and the transient nature of the physical is realised.

THE TRANSIENT NATURE OF THE WORLD REALISED

Insights come from the deepest level of our being. We may spend our life focused on our own perceived needs. At some stage in our growth, we must see that we have experienced most things the world has to offer, yet we still feel unfulfilled. The transient nature of the world does not fulfil our inner needs. The greatest servants of mankind knew this and served others.

Dr. Albert Schweitzer, Nobel Peace prizewinner, gave up his personal life around 40 years of age to serve humanity. He said the following in an interview in 1947, "Today the task is to get the mass of individuals to reclaim their spiritual heritage and so to regain the privilege they have renounced of thinking as free personalities. They must work themselves out of the condition of spiritual weakness and dependence to which they have brought themselves."

You and I must at some point leave this existence. Knowing this, we need to find permanence. Spiritual strength will be found within us. When we find the Inner Light, the truth of the world is seen with new eyes, and personal needs based on the physical world change forever. Permanence will only be found in the experience of Self.

LOVE REPLACES FEAR

In your partnership, or with children and parents, you generally have a feeling of permanence. A comfort zone is built around the denial that it will end one day. We may say that nothing is permanent but most of us turn away from the transience of life with statements like, "how morbid to concentrate on such a negative subject." My answer is simple. When we prepare ourselves for what must happen, we find our focus becomes held in the moment, where we can be absorbed in love. Each moment of life becomes precious. Time for egotistical behaviour, sulking, anger and resentment, are replaced with the desire to be in Love always. Arguments resolve quickly, with a deeper caring for the partner's well-being. The precious moments that we have together put life in perspective when we know that life can end at any time.

A question I ask my students is, "If you had to leave this Earth right now, not being able to say goodbye, what is the most important thing that you wish you could have done before leaving?" Almost always the answer has something to do with expressing their love to a dear one. What more can I say? Remind yourself every day of the impermanent nature of this world so that it loses its grip on you. Building your inner life on spiritual values will bring peace and happiness. Once the well of your heart has been reached, nothing else can quench your thirst, because when you serve another soul with love, you serve All.

ജ

Relationships can crush you, but just what is getting crushed is hard to determine until you get it right.

LESSON 9

Detachment
Being Totally In Love, Is To Know That There Is No Separation

SEPARATION IS IMPOSSIBLE

Master Jesus assured us that he would be with us forever, as close as if we held out our hand, he would be right there. In this statement we are being told that while we experience different conscious states, live in different dimensions, experience various roles in different lives, separation is impossible. We are One and will always be that. Separation is an illusion.

Separation is another tool of the ego for fear-based control. We will never be separated from the souls we have come to know and love as family and friends. Separation is a fear-generated illusion. We move in and out of different conscious states and temporarily lose conscious contact with our loved ones. We weep for those who we cannot, in truth, be separated from. Detachment frees us from pain born of illusion and fear.

ATTACHMENT

Attachment is born of delusion. We believe we need a certain person or situation or possession to be happy and fear is the immediate result. Fear that we will lose them and be devastated.

Life can be likened to a play. When an actor exits the stage another enters. An actor may re-enter in another role or will act again in a different play. When we are in Love - meaning we love every soul as we love ourselves - the change of actors will not affect our enjoyment of the play. When we focus on one actor and believe the whole play revolves around them, then the play is ruined for us when their part is over. As we begin to recognise the importance of each actor and their role, we do not feel the great disappointment and loss as one leaves and another enters. All have equal value.

LOSS IS IMPOSSIBLE

The fear of loss is our greatest fear. Loss of a partner, loss of life, loss of children, loss of job, loss of home, loss of security. It is always the fear of loss. We are persuaded to buy things by advertisers and marketing experts based on our fear of loss; loss of prestige, loss of opportunities, loss of income, loss of security in old age, loss of education for your children, loss of entertainment, loss of responsible government. This is the greatest weapon that governments and private institutions use to induce you to vote for them or to buy some product. Our self-made reality has to be seen for what it is and loss of fear is the way out of it.

Fear and attachment go together. If we feel detached from people close to us, then we fear being judged as cold-hearted and uncaring. Yet being detached is knowing that we are together forever in many forms, on our journey to a conscious joining with Universal Consciousness where the individual experience, as we know it, no longer exists.

It is like a child visiting a friend and discovering a toy that specially attracts them. The child plays with it all day and becomes very attached to that object. When the time comes to go home, the parent explains to the child that the toy must be left behind because it does not belong to them. Then the unhappiness begins as the attachment is broken. The child does not understand that it must let go, only that it wants to keep the toy. The child knows that it has to go so the pain of breaking the attachment is great. The more the child hangs on, the greater the pain.

Detachment comes with the sure knowledge of life everlasting and seeing our roles over many lifetimes. The nexus to break is the fear of loss. Your loved ones can no longer die or disappear or their light be extinguished. They are eternal and will go on forever. Stop fearing their loss, it cannot happen. We fear loss because we love someone for our own sake rather than theirs; we are dependent on them for our happiness. Pain and suffering is inevitable if this is the foundation stone of our love. To love another for their sake is freeing and brings less suffering when the physical parting comes, as it will and must. When we love for our own sake, attachment is strong and painful to break. Loving someone for their own sake still causes pain when they leave but will not crush you, leaving a victim wallowing in self-pity. We mourn the passing of those close to us but we must finally learn to detach ourselves from the play.

PLAYING THE DETACHMENT GAME

Detachment is one of the most important lessons because, in truth, there is no separation. However, our ego has ways to keep us off balance. When we gain any measure of detachment, the ego plays its first card. guilt. The ego tells us, you are not detached, you are just plain heartless. We succumb and our emotions overawe us.

Even though we love our family deeply, we still sink into guilt. We then attach ourselves to the family drama and become involved in rescues and family politics, hurt others and get hurt ourselves. When we try detachment again as the path to peace, the ego plays its second card, fear of loss. You can now choose love and compassion by practising forgiveness. When you see the ego's game plan, you can step out of it and be free. On a physical or practical level, you can decide when and how to help family and friends. That's your lesson.

Divorce brings its own painful lessons. I share one experience. After my own separation, a drama unfolded which resulted in my family taking sides. I was alone with much anger directed at me. Very angry letters were sent to me from my then wife. The temptation to defend myself was enormous. But, of course, this would have flown in the face of my own teaching. So I worked hard with forgiveness and love.

Over the next year communications were severed but I continued to send birthday cards and other small greeting cards from time to time. I refused to put any energy except love into the situation and remained detached. One year later, almost to the day, my daughter contacted me. The lesson is always the same. Divine Consciousness will sort it out if you will only allow it. forgiveness-love-compassion-detachment. Fuse those words into your consciousness.

ꕥ

We come and we go with no earthly possessions, yet we hold onto that which we must let go of. To contemplate the transience of the world is to force us to consider reality. Which is real and permanent, the inner or outer world or both?

LESSON 10

Fear
The Absence Of Love

THE CHOICE IS OURS

Fear is a choice, just as love is a choice. What we think or feel at any given moment is a choice. Realising this we can then set about becoming masters of self – the ultimate objective, the very reason for existence. Fear has been, and still is, the popular choice of the planet as a whole. We hold fear about our future, our health, our partner's health, our children's health, our job, jobs for our children, about paying the mortgage, car repayments, premature death, wars, famine, about being robbed, mugged, the list is endless.

We are not content to just worry about ourselves, we worry and hold fear about the welfare of others around and add to the fear generated in the world. The group consciousness holds enough fear about the welfare of the planet to destroy it without the assistance of pollution.

When enough fear is generated, we have war; we unleash our anger at another country. Anger is a defence against revealing our fear. By acting fearfully we leave ourselves open to attack by an aggressor. We retaliate with fear-based righteous anger. We may kill, claiming God is on our side. Wars are fought in the name of peace. Every war or act of aggression has started as a thought in someone's mind. Who helped create it?

When we feel anger, our heart aches, telling us to stop. Our ego speaks loudly for us to continue. Here is the free will that we asked for and received. We choose the next scene, it can be ugly or beautiful. Our power to create our next reality lies in our hands at this moment. This is the battleground where the true hero stands out. To triumph over our emotions makes us strong and lights a path for others to follow. In these moments of victory we draw close to our true nature, dimmed for so long behind the ego that we struggle to believe that we can achieve this.

BY EMBRACING LOVE, FEAR MUST GO

You are the beginning and the end of all that is. Within you, there lies the dormant power to change anything. Yet we find it difficult just to change our mind. We can reject the long held belief that we need to be fearful and instantly change our conscious experience of life. The power is ours, given to us when we were created, to use for good. But we chose fear and darkened the planet for millenniums. How many more lifetimes do we need to get it right?

FEAR IN THE BODY

The Divine Light will enter by invitation. It's your choice. When trauma occurs, the whole body reacts. Shock lodges in the cellular memory and is carried by your body from then on, long after the trauma is forgotten or suppressed. Deviations in the body tell the story to the alert therapist. Fear-based emotion that is held in the body presents itself as pain, numbness, weakness, malfunction or a myriad of other manifestations in body and mind.

If you think that the past is the past, then let me tell you that the past is the present.

Remembering that there is only love or fear as conscious

states, then all of our body-mind deviations are fear-based, even though they present themselves as various symptoms. There are many wonderful books written on this subject and I will not deal with it here.

Fear is now in every cell of our bodies and needs to be washed away. By opening our hearts and minds to Creation and letting Love determine our thoughts, words and actions, fear must eventually leave us. Love is eternal, fear is not.

FEAR ON THE PLANET

Fear has saturated the planet and life upon it. Animals are slaughtered in the most fearful of circumstances and then fed to us. We eat the cells of fear saturated meat. Animals are experimented on in the most dreadful ways and generally treated with a total lack of love. Our living forests are brutally chainsawed and devastated.Our oceans are pillaged in fear that each country may not get enough to meet their needs.

Excess foods are dumped in fear that the markets may slump if there is a perceived over supply. There is fear that the currency may rise to high or fall too low on the money markets. Insurance companies feed your fear about accidents, lingering illness and premature death, or having nothing for your retirement.

Governments trade on fear so that you will not vote for the other political party. Drug companies feed your fear of disease and produce more pills and potions than we could ever need to calm our fears, while making handsome profits, yet we still get sick as more and more viruses are discovered. Fear has become the normal state of human consciousness.

FEAR IN THE GROUP CONSCIOUSNESS

Imagine a great, swirling mass of thought energy - dynamic, alive and forever changing shape, size and vibration along with a corresponding colour. This energy form subtly influences all that comes in contact with it, that is everyone and everything on the planet. This ever-changing energy cloud is influenced by the group thought energy of the human race. On a more local level, countries have their own energy fields produced by the inhabitants. At an even more local level, the cities and towns are surrounded by energy manifested by the people who live there, and this is experienced as "different" by people passing through.

The group energy of a town is the sum total of the thought energy produced by its population. In balance, most towns have a fairly harmonious energy field, because the mixture of low vibrations and higher vibrations produce a liveable energy for most people. However, we accept less than what we can have—a life of love, joy and happiness where fear cannot dwell.

This shows us that separation from our neighbours' problems is impossible. The town is affected by the greater mass of the country's thought energy and the country by the world's. You can see how your thoughts affect the entire world indirectly and more directly, the town and street where you live. The change of world consciousness starts with you. Exchange your fear for love and watch your children and partners change. You are a miracle worker but refuse to believe it. Being totally in Love is to be without fear.

DEALING WITH FEAR

There are wonderful publications available with exercises on how to deal with fear. My recommendation is find one that feels right and apply the principles in your life. At some point you will discover that unfounded fears rarely become reality, and so a gradual letting go begins.

This letting go is like the child on the springboard, hesitating to jump into the water. It is fear that holds them back.

Often, we cannot say specifically what it is that we are afraid of, so we come up with a list of excuses for underachieving or not doing what we are capable of. In other words, we rationalise through our ego why we cannot do something. It makes us feel better for a while, we have avoided facing the very lesson that will make us free spirits – that of breaking through the wall of fear that we manufactured in the first place, our self-made prison of illusion.

HOW I DEAL WITH MY FEAR

Like you, my body and mind has been saturated with fear. Fear, like any other internal experience, gets a grip on us through the thoughts we hold. Some time ago I accepted that my thoughts were not ME. The thoughts that came to me, I decided, were the ones that I attracted, and I gave them life and form. Because I was part of Creation, I also had powers of creation. I just did not understand them or really know how to use them correctly. So I held on to hard thoughts that were fear-based. I judged and held on to every experience I had, focusing thought power into it until it manifested in my physical body as pain or disease. After releasing large amounts of fear on the healing table, I decided to stop using my Divine gifts for negative purposes.

Catching fearful thoughts before they got a grip on me and dissolving them in positive ones is not a new idea, but it works well. The secret of doing this well is in practising it until you master it (being mindful). You and I choose our thoughts and then experience the reality that comes with them.

CHANGE YOUR FOCUS AND FEAR WILL GO

When we look upon the world and everything in it with attachment, we will always live in fear. As we gain inner sight of the true Self, the Soul that is us, and of eternal Consciousness, fear will go from us. We cannot have dual vision where one can share both the inner sight and external sight. As our inner sight develops and we see who we are, the outer world shows its transience and impermanent nature to us. We have deep experiences of truth, powerful insights that usher in a change of consciousness.

STAY FOCUSED ON YOUR DIVINE NATURE

Whatever you empower in your life becomes your reality. Keep your attention on the inner Light that you are. In the impermanent nature of this world, the inner Divinity is the anchor that will hold you safe in the storms of life that will wash over you. Whatever is outside of you will change or go away. Attachment to these will bring fear because you know that they are impermanent.

UNIVERSAL LAW

Like attracts like. By holding the fearful thoughts of anger, intolerance, greed, lust, selfishness, egotism, and similar negatively, you attract more of it to you, which influences you to stay in that cycle of thinking. And you are adding to the overall negative energy of the planet. Negativity will surround you and encourage you to continue along this path of self-destruction. You are a Divine being. You are not weak and helpless, you are powerful and have at your command all the power of the universe.

CHANGE YOUR MIND AND CHANGE YOUR EXPERIENCE

The negative reality we create for ourselves is not part of the Divine plan. If you want some disaster to strike, all you have to do is focus on it long enough with enough energy, and you can manifest it. Within us we have the power to have whatever experience we want, it's our choice. Re-focus into Love and change your experience.

ꝏ

We know that we limit our love, because we are moved to destroy that which appears fearful to us. Fear in the past has robbed us of our spiritual life, to embrace love we must step across the abyss of fear. The abyss is dark and filled with terror and taking this step into love we must trust completely. We grasp onto what we have, until we find that the abyss does not exist.

LESSON 11

Equanimity Of Mind
Expectations Create Imbalance

THE MIDDLE WAY

Equal mindedness is to be free of expectations. Effort is required to achieve a reasonable level of competency. If we do not achieve at least some degree of equanimity, we will be at the mercy of random emotional states.

Yesterday we felt wonderful, today we feel bad because of a short phone call or message or some vague feeling that we cannot quite identify. Our equilibrium is fragile at best, we never know when we are going to be happy or sad. In the middle of an emotional storm, we are totally at the mercy of our feelings. We are like leaves in the wind, swirled about helplessly.

A part of self-mastery is to learn how to control our emotional body. Equal mindedness is necessary for us so that we may have a peaceful and happy life. By controlling our expectations and reactions, we in no way diminish our enjoyment of people and experiences.

CONTROLLING EMOTIONS

Control of the emotional body requires mental effort. Controlling our thoughts is the only way we can control our emotions. Suppressing emotions is not the way. As we react to a given set of circumstances, our emotion rushes in and becomes all consuming, flooding our consciousness. In our unmanaged state, we allow the emotion to dictate our reaction and become victims of apparently uncontrollable states of mind. Not feeling the emotion is not the objective, but to feel, experience and control is.

Children cannot control their emotions and scream when things do not go their way. Later, as adults, we suppress the scream and pretend all is well. Both situations are out of control, but the child deals with their problem and then gets on with life.

When an emotion floods in, deal with it as if it were a thought, by seeing it, feeling it, but not letting it dictate your reaction or letting it ruin your peaceful state. An emotion is no more you than a thought is. You are not that emotion, you are a loving centre of peace confused about who you really are and who believes that emotions are you. And you react accordingly. This makes us highly unstable. Our unbalanced emotional body affects our physical body, sometimes to the point of making us feel ill or out of control. We may completely give in to our emotions and later deeply regret our actions.

The mental body cannot function because emotions flood our consciousness and clear thinking becomes impossible. The mental body controls all our other bodies. If we do not begin to gain control of our emotional body by the mental body, we cannot master ourselves. A feeling of peace and recognition of the opportunity to practise equanimity by being mindful of what is going on behind our defences will bring us control. Judgement is a doorway through which we allow emotions to run wild. At all times we can choose our thoughts. Like an unbroken horse, our mind will not give in easily. Gentle persistence is the way, and loving tolerance of yourself as you learn mastery.

SOME HINTS ON CONTROLLING EMOTIONS

- Quickly perceive the incoming emotion as a thought form that is either allowed to make you its prisoner or not.
- Feel the emotion as you would feel water for a bath, objectively testing its intensity.
- While sensing the intensity of the emotion, maintain control by controlling your breathing and relaxing your body.
- Go deeper inside and see what it is stirring up within you.
- Recognise and release what you are hiding.
- Allow others to fully express themselves.
- Know that any anger directed at you is an internal experience of theirs.
- See the need of your friend to control and allow them full expression.
- Wait for all the hostility to calm down before offering your feelings.
- At all times honour the other's needs and rights.
- Find some truth in what they are saying and give it full consideration.
- If the reason for their anger does not agree with you, don't let your ego tell your friend. You are trying to score against them if you do.
- If you are truly in Love with your friend, what is it you wish to win from them? And what value to you are the spoils?

Determine whether or not the other person actually wants you to comment. Once they have expressed themselves ask them if there is anything else they want to say. Most importantly, repeat to yourself:

> If I defend myself I am attacked. But in my defencelessness I will be strong, and I will learn what my defences hide.
>
> – *From 'A Course in Miracles'*

Whilst experiencing an emotional situation, breathe into, and release ego- based defences that occur. Hold emotions in check and allow calmness to prevail. It is surprising how, when we listen attentively with love to another's fear, we see the true reason for their attack, and in that honouring we can give understanding. Resist any comment until they have calmed down. Often there is no need to comment at all, as it is an experience that they are having and it has little or nothing to do with you. Be detached and observe. Watch your own defences and learn. Every victory that we have over our emotions is sweet indeed.

Buddha promoted the "middle way", balance in all things. Buddha, like all masters and teachers, exhibited balance in thought, word and deed. Buddha advocated the middle way after years of meditation. Highs in life are followed by lows. It is better to be moderate in our reactions as we never know what the next experience is going to be like. To be even handed in our reactions to our emotions keeps us calm and balanced in our interactions. This calmness honours you and others. Highs increase expectation and crush us when these expectations are not fulfilled. And then we are negative until we are able to get over the disillusionment. We climb out of the low and prepare for another round of highs and lows.

When we react excessively, we spend our lives on a roller coaster ride, believing we get the maximum enjoyment from the "ups" of life when compared to the depressions of the "downs. The calm person who practises equanimity constantly enjoys the experiences that come their way and has few lows. Until calmness is achieved, we will not experience the well of peace within that allows our Inner Light to shine. Meet adversity with the same state of mind as pleasure, with calmness and balance.

LETTING GO OF EXPECTATIONS

Pushing the thoughts from our minds that generate high expectations and depressing lows helps us maintain inner calm, brings clear thinking and a feeling of constant well-being. Your reality is transformed by a stable energy, and life becomes a wonderful experience. We enjoy the company of a calm person, their stable aura. To have expectations about healing sessions may be a continuous source of disappointment when we envisage an outcome. We do the healing and let go.

Letting go of expectations will save you fluctuations of your mental state and reward you with a feeling of peace. This step is an important one towards self-mastery. Pulling your energies back into the moment helps to control expectation. Letting go of expectation does not diminish the enjoyment, but does the opposite. We enjoy more of life than ever before and hold a feeling of peace that we only briefly experience. In this peace we fully realise the Truth in all things.

ஜ

You can watch a movie and be emotionally swayed back and forth by the characters and the plot, then let life do exactly the same thing to you. Which is real and lasting, the movie or life? Which scenario presents us with the lessons we need and is there any difference between the two?

LESSON 12

Foresight and Compassion
Fools Rush In, Where Angels Fear To Tread

ATTRIBUTES OF THE WISE

These qualities are found in a pure heart; to have the patience and foresight not to act impulsively when in the midst of an emotional whirlpool shows strength and wisdom. We may be endowed with many spiritual gifts and be well pleased with ourselves and our capabilities, but these gifts mean nothing when we act without foresight and compassion.

The ability to see the results of our intended actions is a gift that will enable us to live without remorse. Coupled with compassion for others, we will look at the results of our actions and how they may adversely affect others. Thus the wise person will save themselves and others much pain. Compassion for others places them above us. By being selfless, we put others' needs above ours and offer the highest service there is to the world.

OTHER PEOPLE'S NEEDS

In meeting others' needs, ours are met to the full. The inner fulfilment we receive by serving others surpasses all other experiences on this physical plane. Compassion for others is to put their needs first before making decisions or reacting without careful consideration. In order to fulfil another's needs, it may be necessary to stay out of their life and allow them to experience what they need to. Or it may be that your timely intervention will save great pain and they will still learn from the lesson.

The decisions facing us require great foresight. Our use of foresight must be free of random emotions, because emotions will colour our thinking and almost assuredly complicate or delay a much-needed experience for the very person that we want to see move ahead. By combining foresight and compassion, everyone around you will be spared from thoughtless acts, which hurt and distress. The needs of others are our needs. If people around us are unhappy with our actions, we will soon be without friends. It is far better to give love and withdraw quietly than to act mindlessly when confused with fear or emotion that is out of control. We get our innate need to help others confused with our ego's need for recognition. We can get caught up in the "feelgood" syndrome and lose sight of what is the best thing we can do for the other person, which may well be nothing. And in that lack of action we learn our greatest lesson. To continually shield a young adult from life is like sending a child out to cross a busy and dangerous road, because sooner or later you will not be there to guide. Foresight and compassion develop wisdom – from wisdom comes right action. Right action can sometimes be no action. Right action can also make us fearful and be difficult to carry out. Only you know what you need to do in that moment.

THE COMPASSIONATE HEART

Anti-social behaviour is not from a person's Divine self. But in the heat of the moment it is easy to look through the eyes of fear and condemn others. A compassionate heart is not ruled by the ego, but through Love, which resides in every heart waiting for the day when it replaces fear.

Compassion comes with persistence... persistence in the knowledge that our Divine nature will override fear in our life. By being steadfast in our belief that Divine Light resides in our heart, and empowering that belief in our day-to-day actions with Love, we will see miracles. Miracles are there, but we do not see them. Our new eyes are those of compassion.

Mother Teresa was asked how she felt as she collected lepers and the sick, sometimes carrying them in her arms back to her hospital. Mother Teresa said something like "I see God having a bad day." You don't have to be very intuitive to know what eyes she was looking through. Negative behaviour is dealt with by the law and the doer's own inner pain, we do not have to put up with negative behaviour or love it. These souls are still your equal as created. Within each person an illuminated Soul is waiting to find expression.

When a person is struck down through bad fortune or illness, it is not hard to find compassion for their plight in our hearts. But when a person has done wrong in our eyes, behaved anti-socially, and is then struck with misfortune, we feel avenged and righteous. By harbouring our anger for those we feel have wronged us, we allow fear to take over once more. Our Divine self is buried under our ego once again. To dishonour ourselves in this way is a sin against our true nature and Divine Consciousness. Love and compassion for all parties in the play of life frees you from self-imposed limitations about who you are. You are far greater than fear and anger.

In our hearts we feel compassion for the victims of crime, accidents and disease. We hold out a helping hand and extend a loving attitude. We don't stop to judge the victims past, we just step forward to help. At that moment if they told you of their past wrongs, would you deny them and walk away? Be honest with your answer. We can be cold and hard and feel good about a wrongdoer's misfortune, yet feel compassionate for another we see as a victim and not care about their past. Judgement leads us on a pathway of illusion and fear. Compassion cannot manifest where there is judgement. True compassion for others knows no boundaries. Mother Teresa did not ask if someone she carried was a murderer or saint, she loved them all for in each soul she saw God. Discernment or foresight with our thoughts, words and deeds, and compassion for others, will mark you as having great wisdom and kindness and you will gain from the karmic law of reaping what you sow.

Sometimes through lack of foresight and compassion, the ego may use an argument that runs something like 'its not the money, it's the principle'. The ego may not, in this instance, worry about a physical or material loss, but about a loss of face. We take the moral high ground to hide the fear of loss. Or we may possess something that is valueless to us but may well benefit another if we were to pass it on. With compassion we see that generosity and giving will result in what we may not need being of use to others. Yet we harbour a feeling of 'If I can't have it then they can't' and justify this by believing we are in the right because the possession was ours in the first place. There may even be a tussle or war involved but if we give up willingly then we are aware of the outcome beforehand and accept the result. In other words, is it better to fight for half of something or to give the whole to another so that it may benefit them? Will the spoils of an ego-driven victory be of any value to your Inner Light or Spirit? A compassionate heart works with love and is always aware of the transient nature of life.

ꝏ

Compassion demonstrates clarity, Truth judges not and is understanding.

LESSON 13

Truth : The Province Of Light
In All Things Truth Must Prevail, Thereby Freeing The Human Spirit

LIES BIND US IN A WEB, TRUTH SETS US FREE

In the half-light of "white lies", we were taught and continue to teach our children how to lie. We teach them by letting them witness us lie.

The ego explains away our actions and justifies them. White lies lead to greater lies just as soft drugs lead to hard ones. The justification for the big ones is: "I just could not tell them the truth, it would hurt them so much," whereas our own fear of the consequences made us lie. Our ego always finds a reason for lying, because while we are in fear it controls us. Sooner or later others will see the chains with which we encircle ourselves by lying.The later the discovery of the lies, the greater the pain and consequences. We may, if we wish, carry the mantle of truth easily and openly. Fear will still arise, but can be overcome swiftly and easily with practice.

USING TRUTH AS A WEAPON OF THE EGO

We use truth to hurt others. A common statement is: "I told them the truth and they did not like it one bit. They won't forget that in a hurry." Using truth in a hurtful manner for revenge is the same as deliberately saying hurtful things for selfish reasons.

There is always a way to speak honestly and gently to your brother or sister to avoid unnecessary hurt. Hurting another by speaking truthfully is sometimes unavoidable, but you do not have to hand out a verbal beating.

THE EGO AND HOW IT PROTECTS YOU FROM THE TRUTH

Our negative judgement of others can never justify our secretly speaking ill of them. When we judge another, we tie our energy to their's until we have learned our lessons. Honouring them and yourself by being loving and tolerant frees you and them energy-wise and physically. Have you noticed how a negative situation stays with you until you let go of it?

No thought, word or action is secret. You place your thoughts and words into the universe unaware of how and when they will return to you. Before you send them out it is wise to ensure they are of the quality you would welcome back.

When we have released negative words and they return to bite us, the ego looks for a scapegoat. We always find someone who returns the energy we created, but we do not want to take responsibility for our words and actions. To save face and avoid shame, our ego hangs the other for our crimes and denies we could have said or done such a thing.

We must take total responsibility for our actions. No matter what happens to us, we caused it with fear motivated behaviour. No matter how another person appears to us through our delusion, remember it is our delusion not theirs. Spiritual responsibility has great challenges and lessons for us and Truth is the most frightening for the ego because it will set us free.

CIRCUMSTANCES WHEN NOT SPEAKING TRUTH-FULLY IS LIVING TRUTHFULLY

If you know something which is the truth but would greatly hurt another, not speaking about it does not make you a liar. To avoid unnecessary hurt to another person, carefully chosen words can impart the truth. You do not have to lie and you minimise the hurt to your brother or sister.

When a situation is unavoidable where speaking truthfully can be hurtful, speak lovingly and gently, just as you would wish to be treated. You will bring no joy to your heart by hurting anyone, even your perceived enemies. When we strike out at our brothers and sisters, we strike ourselves too, in our hearts. There is no separation. Wear the mantle of truth humbly and lovingly. Look to His Holiness The Dalai Lama for inspiration. Speaking the truth is not a burden, it lightens our load and sets us free. When others know of all your actions and truth is your way, you become fearless.

ஐ

Fear prevents truth. Fear can be there and truth still prevail, so why do we choose fear? Is there such a thing as a white lie? If a statement needs justification, does this mean it cannot stand alone? Truth needs no embellishment of any kind.

LESSON 14

Guilt
The Thief Of Spiritual Life

STRICKEN WITH GUILT

Being stricken with guilt makes us sick to the stomach with fear. Guilt is such a wonderful tool of control for the ego that it will not easily let you go. That is why this lesson comes later in this book.

Our spiritual growth pivots on three lessons in life:

1. Forgiveness.
2. Self-forgiveness.
3. Letting go of guilt.

Each one of the lessons requires you to drop judgement of yourself and others. There are many other lessons to learn, but these three are the basis for mastering all the others. Let's explore each more closely.

Forgiveness of others is essential to let go of stored anger and the emotional pain resulting from it which dishonours ourselves and other souls.

Self-forgiveness is essential so that we can begin our journey into spiritual freedom.

Letting go of guilt brings back our self-worth and breaks

karmic ties. When guilt is dispensed with, the fear-filled energies binding you to another soul will dissipate. Those fear-based energies will be replaced with loving ones.

Guilt will grip you in a vice of fear that is relentless and destructive, squeezing the life out of you. Guilt will be released when the lesson it holds has been fully learned.

THE GUILT WE CARRY

Most of us carry guilt relative to our individual experience of life and our personal reality. For instance, not returning too much change given at a store may cause a person tremendous guilt until they feel compelled to make amends by returning it. Another may take over a company, strip its assets, put staff out of work, cause financial ruin for personal gain and feel no guilt.

Guilt is a personal and individual experience. Often when we share our feelings of guilt with others, we find the other person wonders why we even bother with it, and we may feel the same with their experiences. Guilt cannot be categorised and a value table produced so that we can all feel guilty with the same intensity for similar deeds.

Sometimes we feel guilt and our perceived victim wonders what on earth we are concerned about? Some carry guilt that has lead them to suicide. Yet others are unconcerned over a similar action.

We cannot truly understand another person's feeling of guilt. It is a very personal inner experience, the intensity of which can only be understood in our own personal reality. This area of self-help sometimes requires the assistance of a skilled therapist.

Unskilled observations about another's actions can be unhelpful. If you carry guilt from the past, it is very important that you are assisted skilfully by an experienced counsellor or loving friend. You need a friend who will not put value judgements on our guilt but show you love and compassion. It is most helpful to release our guilt with the assistance of a friend (professional or otherwise) who will not make light of our burdens, so we can then share them on the deepest level. In this sharing we will unearth the "why" of it all and our loving friend can help us lay down our guilt filled burdens.

Until the lesson is learned without judgement, there can be no release. We pass judgement; there is a part of us that cannot wait for the summary execution, and that is our ego. You are more than this judge or executioner. You are a Divine being, a child of the universe. You are capable of the most loving and compassionate actions. Do not let the ego hang you before you have looked at the evidence, the "why" of your actions.

THE ROOT CAUSE OF GUILT

Fear is the cause of negativity in our life. Fear of disclosure, fear of loss of face, fear of loss of loved ones, fear of other's judgement. Fear of loss of friends, fear of being seen as less than your perceived ideal.

When an action raises fear of loss, guilt follows. To feel guilt, we must fear loss. Without fear, there is no guilt. When we understand why we do things, guilt can be let go of.

Guilt will stay with you as long as you want it to. The fear we hold in our hearts will ensure that. While we continue the dishonouring of others and ourselves we will stay in the ego's grip. If you cannot do it yourself, get help to find out the "why" of the actions you took.

GUILT IN THE HOME

Guilt in the home can manifest from many different areas of family life, the most common being guilt about not being good enough. Case histories about women in abusive partnerships abound. The woman is repeatedly told she is worthless. Along with emotional abuse, there is often physical violence as well. She will stay in that relationship because she believes what she has been repeatedly told. Fear, in the form of guilt, will stop her from taking back her power and changing her situation.

An abusive partnership can work either way. A woman can be far more subtle with emotional abuse than her male counterpart. Abusive relationships all work with fear, with guilt as the result. An abusive relationship can be changed with love and honesty.

The abusive man is also in fear. He needs control because he fears loss of power over his partner, and does not know any other way of maintaining a relationship. He uses anger, an expression of fear, to cover up his own guilt and unresolved past issues. In many ways, he is the greater victim, in as much as his need for love cannot be expressed, because to show it he believes will be seen as weak and he will lose control. His greatest fear and greatest need are the same, to give and receive love. Low self-esteem, which is very common among people in all areas of life, is the breeding ground for feeling guilty about your perceived lack of achievement.

A husband or father who has become unemployed and dependent on his wife supporting him and the children, creates pressures through feelings of low self-esteem that can break up a marriage. This translates into anger and violence against the very person who is trying to provide for him and his children. The anger comes from resentment over his feelings of loss of power. Projection of guilt onto our children is the most horrific of all. Guilt in the home comes from all things that are not born from truth, purity and selflessness. The damage we do is enormous.

GUILT IN THE PARTNERSHIP

This situation is rife in our society because of the deterioration of spiritual values. We are bombarded from an early age with sex, violence, drugs, and a wide variety of antisocial behaviour. By the time a marriage or partnership is entered into, either one or both partners has imbibed self-destructive techniques that lead to the failure of the partnership.

Modern violent movies provide us with role models that glorify aggression, physical and emotional violence, multiple sexual partners, cheating in relationships, deceit and lying as acceptable behaviour fed to young, impressionable minds. An honest, loving and committed relationship is a rarity, not the norm.

Where does guilt come in? Deep within each one of us is our spiritual Self which reminds us of the good within us; the positive values which are within us. The persistent but quiet inner voice reminds us that what we need is truth, honesty and love in our lives and we know this to be true. The most hardened criminal knows somewhere deep inside that that is what they need. Guilt comes from knowing what is right for you, but denying it. The ultimate dishonouring of self is the source of our pain.

GUILT IN THE WORKPLACE

The workplace is no different from our home – we just play our roles with different players and a different script. However, here we have the opportunity to masquerade because the whole cast is doing the same thing, putting on masks.

In the workplace, we can play games with each other by not showing our true selves, and by presenting ourselves as we wish to be seen. This delusion is like a safety valve. Have you ever arrived at work steaming with anger, then, as you walk into the office or factory, immediately put on your happy mask and begun your act? What is extraordinary about this is how well it works. Our anger disappears as if by magic, and the play is on again. We would never treat a fellow worker as badly as we treat our partner or family, or would we? With our new happy face on, we then have the opportunity to feel guilt about what we left behind that morning. We are neither being true to ourselves at home or at work. The constant changing of parts becomes a burden after some years, and we long to put it down.

In a work environment, we struggle to find our true feelings when interacting with others. Defence becomes the norm as we play the game of "I win you lose." Fear becomes the predominating experience when playing bosses and subordinates and flying the ego at the top of the flag pole, proclaiming "look at me, I am the most wonderful, efficient, and loved person in the office."

The opportunities for us to experience guilt are endless and various. The workplace gives us the chance to talk about others behind their backs to enhance our standing with our boss. We can keep information from a perceived rival to make them appear incompetent. There are so many devices we can use at work to play the "I win you lose" game that we can become riddled with guilt as we play these games which, in turn, makes us defensive. We begin to believe this is the real "us" and continue to play out the illusion, dispersing valuable energy (life force) we need for inner strength.

The fear that we generate in our workplace affects everyone. And you take home the games you play at work, and bring to work the games you play at home. You also carry your attitudes from home to work and take work attitudes home with you. We confuse ourselves as to our real feelings to such an extent that we do not know who we are, or where we are going in life. The guilt we create for ourselves at work is usually the first thing we dump as we go in the door at home. Have you ever expressed fear-based accusations of a work mate's incompetency to your spouse, so that you could feel better about yourself? This is the ego in full flight and you in full defence (fear).

MANIPULATION AND CONTROL

At home

We are very good at subtly manipulating our partners and children to do our bidding. We practise the art of high obligation with low pressure to manipulate partners and children into fulfilling our concepts of what they should be doing to make us happy. We teach our partners and children to respond to a look or a word. Behind that look or word hides an implied threat filled with fear.

As children, we probably experienced the same behaviour with our parents. The high obligation technique uses little overt pressure but generates guilt in the person it is applied to. The foundation for this guilt began very early in life with threats like "If I tell Daddy about what you did, he would be very angry, so you had better do as I say." So the process of accumulating secrets and guilt starts.

Parents used ploys like this to hold guilt over us. No wonder we became so good at feeling guilt as we grew up. Many people grow up never experiencing open, honest and loving upbringings.

At work

The immature manager uses guilt or fear to control subordinates. Guilt is a delightful tool for extending working hours; the unsaid word, the quick glance at the clock as someone prepares to go home, the last minute task handed to them as they are clearing up for the day. The early morning email and the one late in the day that demonstrates the manager's loyalty and hard working attitude. These gestures aim to raise your fear of not being good enough, and the accompanying guilt pushes you beyond a fair and balanced expectation of you. The feeling today is that by extending working hours and reducing downtime, such as lunch breaks, productivity is increased.

When you start feeling guilty about going home on time, you have a problem that must be dealt with. I remember when I would stay back and fill in time just to prove a point or demonstrate my loyalty. To be seen leaving on time induced guilt, even when you started early and had completed a good day's work. This needs immediate attention.

Manipulation and control are separate manifestations. Manipulation is a guilt/fear-based tool and control is straight out fear. Manipulation is subtle and covert and sometimes so cleverly done that the employee is hardly even aware of them. The manipulator may himself not be aware of the level of their manipulation.

When this mindset prevails in organisations, the energy of the company is drained away in divisive games of survival and productivity suffers. I have attended management meetings where the major concern was ways of increasing productivity in a divisive and fear-based system. An award winning export company is now closed. The most precious and vital component of that company was the people. Fear perpetrated by the directors drove the company to incredible achievement and a spectacular crash.

The myth that productivity equals hours worked prevails due to inept management theory and practice. This is a simplistic 17th century way of thinking. To produce anything of value or quality, the following must be applied.

- The employee's environment must be fear free.
- The employee's mistakes must be viewed as an opportunity for learning by the supervisor and employee.
- The employee must feel free to take action within their designated areas.
- The employee must be responsible for results.
- The employee must receive due recognition.
- The employee must understand completely what expectations are held of them by the organisation.

These principles are also true for family life; replace employee with partner or child.

Fear used by managers on employees to increase productivity is temporarily successful but eventually counter-productive. The hidden costs of fear-based management are found in the productivity wind-down time before resignation by the employee, and the hiring and retraining time up to full productivity of the replacement.

There is a middle road, where fear is minimised and the employee's productivity recognised and accepted within the requirements of the organisation.

ꙮ

Guilt prevents forward movement of the soul. Atonement is the objective and your understanding of the action is the vehicle in which to travel forward.

LESSON 15

The Thoughts We Think
As The Twig Is Bent, So The Tree Shall Grow

SHARING YOUR MOST SECRET THOUGHTS

We have no secret thoughts. Everything we think is already "out there". Our thoughts are energy just the same as our words. The only difference is that we have not brought them into the physical plane by speaking them. As this dawns on us we first become fearful and guarded. But we all think similar things at different times. You are not evil, we all think those thoughts. Being guarded and fearful encourages us to suppress and deny our innermost thoughts and feelings. This is not the way to deal with them. Open honest exploration of self, while trying to understand the "why", is the way.

You are not being judged, but being loved and encouraged to grow. No matter how far a soul has fallen, or how deep the despair, when the return home is earnestly sought, the pathway is prepared and loving hands come to assist. No soul will ever be forsaken, that is the promise.

THE OCEAN OF EXISTENCE

We live in an ocean of pure energy constantly changing, moving, creating, sustaining, but never still and always renewing and breaking down matter into energy again, ready to recreate. Nothing is lost. Nothing remains the same. Everything is in constant motion. It can be called the Mind of God or Universal Energy, or all that is. That which comes into existence will eventually go again. In this third dimensional reality, everything is temporary, everything must return from where it came. Life is endless – an experience of being reborn into different experiences. Consciousness is the mind of the Divine and can never die. We share in that consciousness, we are at one with all that is. we are that! You and your body are created from, and sustained by, this super intelligent energy. Nothing in this and other planes is separate from It, and is of It in the beginning. All comes from It and returns into It. Nothing is lost. The great formless Consciousness gives life, and in this creation, form and substance. Everything is held together and formed from It. Every molecule is created and given life from It. You can see how the Divine and you are inseparable. Every thought you have, every word you speak and every action you do is known. Now, the term "you are God" may not seem so baffling to you and you can see the sanctity of all life. Everything is part of you, you share the delights of life and the pain. Everything you experience, think, say or do vibrates the energy you share with Creation. You and I are inseparable.

CREATING AND SHARING OUR THOUGHT FORMS

In this ocean of loving Creation our thoughts are unjudged and free. We are not confined or restricted in any way. Our chosen pattern of thinking harmonises with other thought forms of similar vibrations. The harmonising forms are attracted to us by the law of attraction and strengthen our thoughts as they meld with ours. As we continue to think along these lines, more and more thought forms accumulate around us as we create the chosen reality.

The quality of thought determines the reaction of the universe. If idle wishes for wealth occupy most of a person's thinking, nothing will manifest and they will remain in that state. The power behind thought is desire, coupled with will power that stimulates physical action to achieve the goal. If every thought produced results, we would be buried alive in an avalanche of manifestations.

CHANGING YOUR MIND

Once we become familiar with new ways of thinking and begin to attract similar energy, the old ways will release their hold on us.

It takes great diligence and effort to change our way of thinking because we are entrenched in our old way of thinking, using our energy and attracting like energy to us. Our old patterns of thinking and reacting do not leave us easily as we try to develop new thought patterns. Be patient and persistent because it takes time to shift from the old to the new. So be patient with yourself as change takes a little time. Once your thinking changes, you will feel comfortable in your new consciousness.

We change our thought pattern by constantly replacing old for new. Don't dwell on old patterns. You will soon be able to quickly identify a thought as acceptable or as one that is negative. If it is not, replace it with the one you want. Don't let thoughts linger around that are not good for you. The longer they stay the harder they are to get rid of.

There are many systems around to help you stop smoking but there is only one that works, stop smoking! If you dwell on how much you need a cigarette, you will never stop, because you feed these thought forms and continue to attract more. Change your mind, everything else will follow. It is not easy but the rewards far outweigh the effort.

ဆ

If a stray dog enters your house and you refuse to feed it, the dog will leave. You have the power to decide to what and whom you will give food.

LESSON 16

The Words We Speak
Words Are Easily Spoken, But Difficult To Swallow

THE WORD

In the beginning was the word, and the word was with God. That passage from the Christian Bible says a lot. We have discussed thought forms in previous lessons, now consider the extension of thoughts, words.

MISUSE OF WORDS

The power of the spoken word today is grossly misunderstood and underestimated by the masses. We habitually swear and curse, and spend time indulging in aimless and mindless chatter and gossiping. We speak unkind and judgmental words about others. All this drains spiritual energy. This is not to say we cannot be light-hearted and have fun. But mostly we indulge in idle talk with no constructive purpose except to fill up the silence. Useless, pointless stories over a few beers to fill in time. Most of us avoid subjects that are too "deep" or meaningful.

WHY DO WE DO IT?

When we give in to fear, we talk so that we can be like everyone else. Courage is needed to break through the fear and speak about what really matters. And we discover that others respond positively to this, that others too, crave spiritual growth. They may not be conscious of this, but we are born for a higher purpose. Controlling our words is a way to achieve this growth.

THREE POINTS TO CONSIDER

When we converse there are hidden motivations at work:

1. Firstly, the ego is always prompting us to give our valuable opinion to anyone who will listen.
2. Secondly, conversation is an exchange that provides learning for us.
3. Thirdly, there is the spiritual connection that has brought you together, to play out your roles for the highest good of everyone concerned. This needs to be recognised.

When we recognise why we are together and explore the human and spiritual connection being made, we enhance and fulfil our lives in ways we never thought possible. When we share experiences that enhance our spiritual growth it is fulfilling and adds purpose and meaning to every encounter. Don't remain shallow and waste golden moments. It's our choice, to reincarnate again, and again and again and again. Or we can decide to consciously begin our spiritual growth in this life.

MISUSE OF THE GIFT

Words are powerful and can positively affect our growth, health and happiness and communicate loving, positive vibrations in the universe. Words have become throwaway, a symptom of a mindless society. Words are now used to communicate something less, or more, than they actually mean. They are used to mislead and misrepresent. Governments call civilians killed in wars "collateral damage". Politicians answer questions with strings of meaningless phrases that appear to have substance until carefully analysed. Words have become a tool of the corporate world. Instead of mass retrenchments, it is now called downsizing. It is confusing. Many can't cope with the web of deceit even by words and opt out. We have lost our way and it is time to stop and take stock.

To use words carefully, we must rethink how we use and abuse the privilege of speech, and honour this capacity to communicate by carefully choosing what we put into this world through our speech. Chemical pollution is not the only danger we face, words reverberate into the ether and affect the spiritual and physical planes. Take care of what you say and how. History has examples of famous and infamous orators that held sway over millions. President John F. Kennedy spoke with spirit and inspired a nation, Martin Luther King led a nation away from racism with supercharged words that moved the world and pricked the conscience of America.

Idle and useless chatter has little or no psychic or spiritual energy. So to constantly indulge in pointless stories and chatter for the sake of it weakens and debilitates you. Avoiding gossip groups and similar activities keeps you strong and single-pointed. Your precious energy is not scattered and fed off by those who draw energy to themselves by constant chattering. Your mind and aura will remain clear by being focused.

We may choose to speak trivia or truth – constant wisecracking and pointless jokes are draining and have no purpose. Negative words have their own vibration and effect on you.

We may feel anti-social if we stand in our own power and people notice. The pressure to join in is high. It takes strength and commitment to stand in your power. But this is not rudeness. Enough energy is wasted on idle talk, why add to it? Keep meaningless chatter to a minimum for everyone's sake, especially yours. As a messenger of truth your words are important – do not waste them.

A SECRET REVEALED

If you want others to hear your words, work hard with the laws of manifestation. Everything you need to know about powerful speech is in that lesson. When you are ready to see, the information will appear on these pages.

My work involves speaking to large and small groups of people. I use the laws of manifestation always, even in a one-to-one-conversation. There are no exceptions if you want people to listen. Speak only if you have something of value to contribute. Otherwise allow others to say what they need to express themselves. Be a good listener. Develop your listening skills so that you can hear the real message they are trying to convey to you. Mastery of this lesson, as with all lessons, takes time and practice. Persist – it is worth every bit of energy you expend and more.

WORDS RICH IN SPIRIT ACHIEVE MIRACLES

The keys:

1. Words spoken with passion from the heart, that have been born of truth "live in spirit", and add to the positive energy of the planet.
2. When you speak from the heart, with desire and intent for the good of all, others will listen in silence, and be moved at the deepest levels of their being.
3. Charge your words with Spirit, fill your heart with Love, make your intentions known and honourable, and in your hands you will hold the power of Creation.

Choose your words carefully. Dedicate what you say to the inner Light. Pray for guidance.

ꟿ

When I leave this Earth my words and deeds will mark my presence here.

LESSON 17

Spiritual Responsibility
In Time, The Role Of Victim No Longer Suits Us

The choice to "own our stuff ", as we say, brings its own rewards. We no longer need to look for a situation or person to blame for our negative experience. We rarely give credit to others for our good experiences, we generally take credit for these ourselves. While we still see ourselves as victims, we project our negative experiences onto others, not willing to believe that we have created our own reality.

When we take spiritual responsibility, great karmic results are ours. We feel stronger and relinquish a lot of controlling patterns. Our sense of humour and ability to laugh at ourselves and our actions increases. Life has more appeal in a new way.

Our spiritual growth ceases to be a chore. We understand that we can grow and become enlightened beings and enjoy life as well. The Light within us increases steadily as our self-judgement diminishes and we embrace love and learn tolerance of ourselves.

We perceive people and events differently because our changed thinking has shifted our view of reality. Reality is constantly shifting, we can choose to let go of our current views while being responsible for what is happening to us. To re-awaken, we must accept spiritual responsibility.

ACCEPTANCE BRINGS MINDFULNESS

Responsibility ensures that we begin to be aware of our thoughts, words and actions. This is difficult at first but when we realise there is no time limit to achieving this change, we can slowly and methodically get rid of undesirable traits and replace them with loving values.

During an exploration of our consciousness, the real and unreal begin to blur as we re-evaluate our personal reality because our reality continually shifts with our belief systems. What is real and what is unreal? What really matters? And what does not matter? The answer to these questions depends on your current reality, which continuously changes, so the futility of holding on to our concepts becomes clear. Inner peace comes as we realise that our concepts are built on the shifting sands of impermanence.

As we apply these principles, there will be a significant inner shift as the Truth becomes stronger and more available in your consciousness. You will release many formerly held beliefs. Truth comes as an inner experience, beyond intellect or the grasping mind; it is an experience of the heart.

The voice of Truth is subtle and quiet, but its power will change you forever. The reality of Love changes everything, yet in itself it never changes. Only our experience of it changes.

Everything we do on this plane is a substitute for experiencing our inner truth. We have come into a physical body to experience the ultimate truth. The truth cannot be uttered in words, thoughts or actions. It can only be experienced in the heart. When the ultimate experience has been had, no earthly desires will ever hold sway over us. Our Real Nature has been realised.

The material world can be understood by seeing the illusion and simultaneously knowing the Truth. Spiritual freedom is then ours. This world is for self-discovery through experience. When a soul has tasted every experience they need, they will eventually search for the inner truth that brings the ultimate satisfaction of love and joy.

Responsibility is necessary and inevitable as spiritual growth occurs. Becoming reliant on self empowers us by stripping away the barriers to self-realisation. We must look within us for what makes us strong.

We are whole now but do not see it. It is as though our wholeness is obscured by layers of dust. When we wash it away by letting go, we will see our Light and be empowered again. The complexity of our nature and being is not relevant. When we want to read the time, we do not dismantle the watch to see how it works. Our intellect loves complexity, stimulating discussion and theorising without commitment to action. Once we look for Truth, we abandon intellect.

The most direct way within is through the heart. As we journey through our heart, our spiritual centre, our belief systems are challenged until we realise that the ego offers us nothing. It is then that we drop the ego and change. We become spiritually responsible beings without concepts or expectations. We discover who we really are, then claim our place in the Universe as beings of Light.

Being spiritually responsible means many things:

1. We do not tell others what they should do with their life.
2. We offer our own experiences only when we are asked.
3. We give compassion and understanding.
4. We make no claims about our own development.
5. We do not judge another's growth.
6. We honour others' needs.
7. We accept our current situation without judgement.

8. We dedicate our thoughts, words and actions to the Light within.
9. We know that consciousness is a gift.
10. We serve.

ꕥ

Until the doorway of self-responsibility is reached there can be no significant steps taken on the path. When the spiritual beggar inside you is gone, the beggar in the street is gone. You see what your reality allows.

LESSON 18

The Way Home

JOURNEY OF THE HEART

The way is through the heart and it can be reached in many ways. Your life experience in Divine consciousness is shaped by your individual needs. Each soul's journey provides growth and our journeys and experiences are endless. Our universes are limitless and diverse, to see and experience what we need to in order to Love is the main lesson. In each life's journey love is the lesson. To realise this is to enlighten others and ourselves.

At the end of each life, it is the love that we hold in our hearts for the whole of creation that gives us strength to attain the higher realms of consciousness. As we embrace Love more and more, it increases our vibration.

A soul temporarily lost in darkness cannot attain higher planes and exists in a corresponding low vibration between lifetimes. Each life gives an opportunity for the soul to learn and grow, gradually increasing its frequency through learning about love. As our heart gradually opens to our brothers and sisters, the higher vibration of love changes us and cleanses us to become a servant of humanity.

A Master is a true servant. All Masters have served without personal desires, owning little more than the basic necessities of life. They lived to bring Truth to the Earth plane. All their needs were met and they never held on to anything, but gave everything. They had profound Love for creation so that they could not harm anything or anyone. Their Divine consciousness saw everything as One. This is the heart journey.

STEPPING INTO THE RIVER OF LIFE

Your heart speaks to you of love, purity, honesty, selflessness, compassion, and truth. Everything that is uplifting and empowering comes from your heart. All the knowledge you need is in your heart, waiting for you to find it. When sincerity and the desire to become one with the Divine is strong and single-pointed, the Universe answers with great Love. It is as though every book has been read, every road has been travelled, every spring has been drunk from, every stream has been crossed and you are back in the loving arms of creation. You need not have left in the first place, but the journey had its own rewards and purpose.

The purpose of the journey is to attain self-awareness. When we are aware that we are blind, sight is received as a great blessing. When truth dawns, we understand ignorance. Experiences teach us to understand or rediscover our true nature.

There is nothing to know, but to accept the gift of life and love by allowing the wisdom and love of creation to flow through you. This is the river of life; the river of gold and silver which is Divine consciousness that you share. The joy of being still. The freedom that comes as the old ways fall away and you are reborn into the river of Light. Within this river we experience All That Is, yet still experience our individuality.

DRINKING FROM THE WELL

For me, there is no blinding flash of enlightenment but slow adaptation to gradual change. It is an ongoing process, going deeper each time to find trust to let go a little more. You experience subtle changes in consciousness, a gradual awareness that you are finding your way home, as your heart opens more and more to the ultimate experience of unconditional love. You find answers inside you that go beyond logical thought – answers that cannot be expressed in limiting words. You touch the deep knowing that we all have and become who you have always been.

ꙮ

You cannot enlighten through the intellect, nor through spiritual practices that only stimulate the mind. The door of the heart waits for your knock to open. The dam wall you have built must come down in order for the river of life to flow once more.

LESSON 19

The Mind Of God

Illusion, reality, dream, awake, confused, aware, lessons, responsibility, growth, sickness, health, impermanence, temporary, love, joy, happiness, anger, fear, separation, detachment, attachment, freedom, knowledge, ignorance, light, darkness.

It is in everything, and It also fills that which we perceive as nothingness. There is nowhere that It is not. The constant flow of creative consciousness brings to your life, while manifesting around you, everything you need to exist.

What you see, feel, eat, breathe, think, enjoy and love or hate has been given to you. You are the recipient of a force of consciousness so powerful that you cannot conceive of it. Your personal desires are filled impartially and you may not like the consequences. Everything you experience is shared with Divine Consciousness. You may have and experience everything, yet happiness still eludes you. Life cycles continue endlessly and you exercise free will and come to your own conclusions.

Complaining about what you want over and above that which has been given shows ingratitude. To cherish each breath, to love and enjoy each moment, shows gratitude. To stop condemning and to be tolerant brings wisdom to the soul and freedom to the heart.

The Divine Consciousness is the vehicle through which you experience everything. You swim in a river of life, which is part of Creation. Creation's breath fills your lungs and love sustains your conscious life. Divine Consciousness is your life. You are nothing without it.

If you wish to see illusion, you are shown illusion. Truth is seen when all the stains of self have been removed. You will see that you have everything now. Creation provides according to your wants. Give up your wants and allow Creation to provide what you need and you will live in gratitude.

The grasping mind, ego, you created is the cause of your blindness. When you believe you have conquered the ego, it has you in its tightest grip. The wise soul knows the ego cannot be defeated, but it can be subdued in this life by allowing the Light to shine from within you.

Like a fish in a dry river bed, you gasp in your final hours for that which you took for granted. Look around and see what has been given, the precious gift of life. Mourn for the days you have frittered away so that you will seize opportunities now. Resolve to hold the moment in your heart. See the preciousness of every soul because they are also Divine.

You are never more than one moment, one breath, and one thought away from realising Self. Let the urgency and excitement of this moment hold you. Feel the stirrings deep within you of your Love and respect yourself. Welcome yourself home.

ஜ

My safe passage is in the mind of Universal Consciousness when I allow the power of love into my life. In this love I have sanctuary from all of life's storms that wash over me.

LESSON 20

Above All Else Be True To Your Self

If you understood who you really are, self-dishonouring, insecurity, feelings of lack and anti-social behaviour would not exist as they do in your current reality. Your fear dictates your reactions and manifests your faulty belief systems. In this reality, you believe that your experience is real and true.

Your time on earth is made up of birth, life and death, experiences for learning and growth. Each experience is linked to your physical body. These are unchanging laws associated with this planet. There is one way on and one way off.

BIRTH

In order that a soul may experience the gift of life, a physical vehicle results from the act of love by the division of a single cell, a combination of the mother's vibration and the incoming soul. The attachment of each soul to the physical vehicle or body occurs at conception. From that moment on, a living vehicle grows that the soul can bond with on a cellular and spiritual level. During the period before birth, the incoming soul becomes increasingly attached to the growing physical form.

During birth the final union of the body and soul is completed. The veil is drawn and body consciousness begins.

The conscious connection with the spirit world is hidden so that the physical body can connect with the physical world. Dreams and vague inexplicable feelings are all that remain. You are about to begin your greatest adventure.

LIFE

Life is experienced to attain knowledge of Self, or Divine Consciousness. Physical life provides learning that cannot be experienced in any other realm. Every person and situation is the opportunity to see the manifestation of Divine Consciousness.

Through the dual vision of Divine Self (inner voice) and ego, you choose your course of action. Without doubt when you speak or act wrongly, the result will be negative in accord with your words and actions.

Truth and Divinity show the way, while the ego takes you down the road of hard lessons. So listen to your Sacred Self and act on the gentle urging of your conscience. Don't listen to the shouting and hysterical screaming of the ego.

Physical life becomes much easier when we have fun, and accept our lessons well with a happy heart. Find Light in everyone and everything. Bless every day and thank creation for our conscious life.

DEATH

Transition from one state to another, the letting go of physical life, can be hard :

1. We believe this physical experience is of importance, when, in truth, only the lessons learned have value.
2. We believe that people around us are important to our sense of place and belonging.

3. Attachments to physical objects give us a sense of achievement, power and security.

All these concepts are challenged at the time of approaching death. Nothing you can do or say will change this inevitability and we can experience intense fear if we do not have a strong set of values. Fear sweeps through you and the last days and hours become a nightmare. Your arrival on this planet is devoid of physical possessions and so is the departure. Everything you have learned to cherish and hold onto is taken from you when you go.

In physical life we have the opportunity every day to prepare for what must happen. Know that each moment, each breath is a gift of great magnificence. Live with a sense of urgency to enjoy your partner and your family and your daily life and everyone you meet. Be happy and give thanks for the time you have here. When your time comes, you will know that you have done everything in your power to have filled your life and everyone around you with love and joy. Give thanks for a good life. Don't dwell on injustice, or think "why is this happening to me now?" You write the story of your life and reap the results accordingly.

8◌

Above all else be true to yourself. Your True Self waits to be freed so that it can fully express itself.

LESSON 21

Self-Acceptance

Self is Divine. You are part of the Divine plan, part of Divine Consciousness. Beyond body, beyond mind and limiting thoughts, lies the Great Consciousness, ever expanding, permeating everything, and creating everything.

We can liken our existence to being a thought in the Universal mind, being nurtured and held in a Loving Consciousness until our experiences lead us inwards to finally accept what is ours, to merge with the Sublime and know It completely. In order to know light, we must experience darkness. After the heat of the desert, the cold of the mountains is a blessed relief. And we begin again to crave the heat and so it goes through many lifetimes.

Experiencing opposites is the way of learning for every soul, until we accept the experience of unending bliss. We cannot attain the higher realms of unending bliss until we are lead there through experience.

As a teenager, we may have left school prematurely to find work to make money to spend in ways we later consider to be foolish and wasteful. Later in life, when we see a child behaving in the same way as we did, with hindsight we judge this as immature and inappropriate. We had to live the experience and grow in order to judge our past experiences as foolish as must the child we are judging in the present, who has to live through his own experiences.

We cannot live in each other's state of consciousness, as we have not travelled the same path. We cannot live in permanent bliss until we recognise the ego's ability to lure us with empty promises of unfulfilled experiences.

Similarly, our urge to fulfil our needs is insistent until we see the Truth behind the need and then the urge goes away.

Only when we realise that the world offers us nothing permanent, can we seriously look inside for that which will bring us what we crave, eternal peace.

The acceptance of self lies in the experience that Divinity and self are one. Acceptance grows gradually in proportion to the inner experiences or insights that we gain on our journey. To enter the gates of heaven, we need to lay down our defensiveness and let our childlike qualities emerge. The simplicity and beauty of the inner journey escapes us, because we no longer think and act with the simplicity of a child and with the love and forgiveness that is their great power.

ཌ

I am a Divine being.

DEATH'S ILLUSION

The Timing

Our physical experience is given without strings attached. It is ours to do with as we wish. Timing of departure is yours to decide. You live in a physical world full of vehicles, implements, machinery, aircraft, boats and all kinds of activity that is accident prone. A person may subconsciously place themselves where the opportunity to leave this plane of existence increases and sometimes completes their desire to go.

The Method

When the weariness and weight of physical life becomes too much, you can and do create departure through disease or what may appear to be an accident. While we are distressed at a loved one's departure, rarely is the departed one distressed once they have been helped and healed on the other side. Returning to freedom after a tough physical life experience or even a long enjoyable one releases a soul from being focused on the recent past life. The unlimited freedom of the spiritual realms becomes much more interesting and the earth experience fades rapidly along with any attachments to people and possessions. The desire to experience more moves the soul on.

There are always exceptions, generally disillusioned souls believing they need to stay in the recent life for a host of reasons.

The Destination

Your beliefs and state of mind will determine your experience in so-called death as they have in life. Nothing changes. How can it? By some miracle does a murderer suddenly become enlightened by death? Of course not. You and I will find ourselves in a space where our consciousness can sustain us, along with other like-minded souls, wherever that may be, and whoever they may be.

When Jesus said: "I go to prepare a place for you" and referred to "My Father's house has many mansions" it is clear what he was referring to.

EPILOGUE

We have lived many lives and experienced many deaths. The cycle continues. You and I have done everything, said it all, and experienced all that the world can offer. When do you think we might stop all the brutality and unkindness, selfishness and every negative trait that the human race can manifest?

I need what you have and you need what I have, let us share it and dissolve our needs in one unselfish action. Life cannot exist without love. Creation gives us everything we need – a full and loving life. Why do we turn away and let fear grasp our hearts?

By isolating each another and concentrating on our personal needs, we create barriers that cause breakdowns at the grass roots of society and spread from there.

What happens in the world, happens first between two people. There is no other way, this is the root cause. Every action and reaction has a beginning and ultimate end. You and I carry the world's burden on our backs – feeling tired?

Pointing and blaming is short-term limited thinking. The responsibility we carry for the good of people everywhere starts at home, there can be no escape and nowhere to hide from this truth.

Rushing out to fix the world while we suppress or deny our own inner problems is self-defeating. Yes, band-aids can be stuck here and there, but our internal haemorrhage cries out for attention. How easy it is to see others' problems but not our own.

How interesting that a huge rock concert held for charitable reasons was called "Band-Aid". All these activities are wonderful acts of kindness and generosity, the world needs them. But poverty and sickness stay with us, in fact it has increased to proportions that stagger the imagination and leave us feeling powerless and angry. Why?

If you have studied the lessons diligently and thought deeply about your place in the world, the answer is already known to you. There must be thousands upon thousands of charities in this world and more every year, yet the tide of suffering increases. Clearly charity alone is not the answer.

As above so below. The Hindu statement on truth and cause and effect. What is in the spiritual realms is reflected in the physical and the reverse is also true. What is inside you is reflected on the outside. Give out love and peace and love and peace will surround you. Sometimes we get confused, we feel peaceful, yet there is pandemonium all around us. Inevitably, under that peaceful exterior there is still work to be done, otherwise we could not be affected by the pandemonium.

These lessons are a constant challenge, because they are eternal truths spoken about throughout the ages. Nothing is new, just altered so that we can see it through our evolving consciousness.

Love is the only answer to the world's problems. It all starts with you. How strong are you really? Can you forgive easily? Do you see only perfection in everyone?

If you can answer yes to these questions then you have already transcended the physical plane and all its lessons, but if you are like me, still trapped by your ego, then life still has much to teach you.

Egotistically we may believe we are highly evolved enlightened beings on our last incarnation. Can you give up all your material possessions today and work for the advancement of human kind? Most of us go into shock at the thought of it.

When we listen to our heart, this is what we hear.

ꕥ

I am here to live my life and show you the way by example. I am here to live in love and harmony in a physical body and show you many wonderful things. I talk to you of love and demonstrate the love of the Divine to you to take away your fear. What you call miracles are your gifts from the Divine to have and use. I am with you always, as close as you want me to be. I can touch your heart as easily as I touch your hand. Hold out your hand and open your heart and you will know that we have never been apart since the very beginning.